Tell Me No Lies

ROSEMARY SULLIVAN AUSTIN

Order this book online at www.trafford.com
or email orders@trafford.com

Most Trafford titles are also available at major online book retailers.

Photography © Dana Davis / Cover Design © Nermin Soyalp

Printed in the United States of America.

ISBN: 978-1-4120-6778-2 (sc)

Library of Congress Control Number: 2012903779

Trafford rev. 10/25/2012

 www.trafford.com

North America & international
toll-free: 1 888 232 4444 (USA & Canada)
phone: 250 383 6864 ♦ fax: 812 355 4082

To Glenn, whom I will love forever

CHAPTER ONE

SHELLEY LEANED UP AGAINST THE patio column and stared across the aquamarine Gulf waters. "Yes, it was a day just like this one, a magical Florida day. It's so hard to believe that it was 10 years ago!" Her pulse quickened as the memories pushed their way to the top of her consciousness, rousting her out of her dreamy feelings. A rush of images, long forgotten emotions surfaced. "What was I thinking?! How could I have been so reckless that summer of 1985?"

*　*　*　*　*

The small red convertible had been trying to pass for the last several miles. The white Winnebago was traveling sedately at the fifty-five mile speed limit. Low to the road, it completely owned the lane of this two-lane highway.

Headed northward out of Key West, the Winnebago chugged onto the Seven Mile Bridge. The Volkswagen Cabriolet grabbed its chance, speeding past the RV as if it were parked. The long blonde hair of the driver splashed about in the back draft.

"Did you see that, George? That girl must be crazy, passin' on this two-lane bridge and going that fast! The elderly lady shook her head. "Heavenly days, she's outta sight already! Must have been going 70 . . . . Maybe 80."

"It'll be good when the other bridge is finished," the man said, glancing at the parallel span to his left. "Shouldn't be too long. This year, maybe." They rode along silently for a few miles until the woman glanced into her side-view mirror. She straightened in her seat and said, "Look, George! Here comes another one. Look at that car comin' speeding up behind you!" Her head whipped around to enable her to look out the driver's window.

The dark Lincoln Continental swept past them as smoothly as an ocean liner cutting through the waves. Sun glasses glinting, the driver glanced at the motor home.

"Did you notice him, George? Brown suit. And a tie! . . . That hat looked like straw," she said thoughtfully. "Everybody else so casual here. Him so dressed-up like. Never can tell, right?"

"Ayah," agreed George.

It was a lovely day. The breeze that April day soothed the sun's heat. The sun turned the seaweed patches red as they floated in the surrounding waters, mixing with the varied and vivid colors only the Caribbean could be: turquoises, aquas, emerald greens, marine blues. The white beach on either side of southern US I reflected the sun like the snow on a sunny day at Aspen, the differences in temperature emphasized by waving palm trees. It could have been in drab black and white as far as the driver of the little Cabriolet was concerned.

The young woman's amber eyes anxiously flicked a look into the rear-view mirror. Each Key was a milestone. One more step away. One hundred and six miles to the mainland. But he'd come after her. Oh, yes. He'd be after her. But she'd not make it easy for him. "Where is that gas station?!" The young woman glanced at the gas gauge again. With her car's small gas tank, she needed to stop. That hateful Continental could go on forever. "Was it in Damorada or on Long Key?" She knew she was talking to herself, but it was either that or cry, and she wasn't going to cry, dammit! She'd done enough of that.

She'd long since stopped noticing the name of each Key when she finally saw the station on the left side of the road. She made a screeching U-turn across the cut in the divided highway and pulled in on the far side of the pumps. Maybe they would shield her, give her some protection. As she was filling her tank, a camper pulled in on the side of the pumps nearest the highway, completely blocking her from sight. She sagged in relief against her car.

Pulling herself together, she replaced the nozzle and went inside the station. Handing her credit card to the cashier, she said, "I'll get a soda from the machine while you write up my charge."

She flipped open the top of the can and took a long, cool swallow, staring fixedly down the road southward. Her heart caught in her throat as she saw the dark Continental come into view. She backed farther into the gas station's office, but the Continental swooped by like an eagle going in for a kill, dust eddying by the highway the only sign of its passing.

A shudder went through her body. Well, she'd gained some time now. Perhaps even a day. Anything would help. It would give her a reprieve, time to make better plans.

She walked back to the cashier's window to pick up her card.

"If you'll just sign here, Miss Morgan . . . ."

'Miss Morgan!' Her heart sank. How did he know her name? . . . Of course, her card! How she wished that this station had pay-at-the-pump and no one would have to know her name.

"That's a good looking car. Volkswagen Cabriolet, isn't it? Don't see many of them. How's it drive? Get good mileage, do you?" the friendly cashier rambled on.

"Yes. Very nice. Good mileage," she nodded, reaching for her card.

"Pretty name, Shelley Morgan," the good soul continued on.

"Yes, thank you." She reached for her card again.

For a second time the camper saved her. As the driver came in to pay for his gas, she left quickly.

Shelley backed the convertible away from the pumps and into the shade of a huge fir tree. She'd have to think. How could she be so dumb?! Well, she'd not park her car where it could be easily seen next time, that's one thing. For another, no more credit cards. She'd get money from the ATM. That way she could pay cash everywhere. It would take time to trace her through a bank, and by then she'd be long gone.

O.K. Next point, where was she going? Not north toward Miami. No. That's where they'd expect her to go. She'd left his house in such a hurry this morning; she'd had no time to plan. Shelley rubbed her forehead. The slight headache must be from not having anything to eat today. She grimaced to herself. Tension had nothing to do with it, of course.

She could take care of one part of the headache. There was a large inn on Key Largo. No one would notice one more traveler in a large hotel dining room.

Then she'd head for Florida City and Homestead, the gateway to both the Keys and the Everglades. Right! The Everglades! She'd head west over the Tamiami Trail through the Everglades! Not much traffic there this time of year. Visitors stick to both coasts. Maybe she'd stay overnight in Naples. Yes—a big impersonal hotel. And, best of all, there would be banks in a city of that size. Once she got some money, she'd pick up a few pieces of clothing. She'd left almost everything behind in her hurry to escape. But her package was safe! No worrying about that now. The important thing was to get away.

Let's see . . . . She should put the top up on the convertible; make it look more like other cars so it wouldn't call as much attention to itself. A convertible, and red at that, really would stand out.

Then, food. It was about forty miles to the Inn near Key Largo, a little less than an hour. Time to get started. At least she wouldn't have to speed the way she had before.

After putting up the top on the car, Shelley pulled carefully onto the highway leading south, looking for a way over the median strip. Upon reaching a crossover road, her turn was much quieter and more decorous than the one that had spun her into the gas station. Things would be easier now that he was ahead of her. They'd be smoother. She could move more quietly in her mind, at least for a while.

Continuing northward at a more leisurely pace, Shelley began to enjoy the beautiful day. Now that she had the time to notice, she could sense that each Key had its own personality, its own atmosphere. When she had first gone down to Key West, she'd roared through the darkness, so upset that she'd barely seen anything other than the road in front of her.

Her thoughts drifted to her reason for having gone to Key West in the first place, and to her captor. Former captor, that is. Even now her heart leapt and her breathing accelerated. Could

TELL ME NO LIES

it be true? Prisoners falling in love with their jailors? Shelley knew a lot about computers, but psychology left her cold.

Nevertheless, Dirk Gentile was the handsomest man she'd ever seen. He was tall, muscled like Adonis, but darker than any Greek god she could imagine. With his silver-grey eyes and crooked smile, any woman would have been mad for him. Shelley had fought him and his attraction for five of the seven days she'd been "detained," as Dirk had put it. But when she fell, she did a great job of it. Just thinking of the glowing bronze tan on those magnificent shoulders . . .

In the midst of her reverie, Shelley suddenly saw the inn. She slammed on the brakes. The car behind swerved to pass in a blare of Klaxton horns, the driver glaring and mouthing unfriendly words. She sat and trembled while the traffic cleared before she backed up slowly to turn into the driveway of the inn. She parked the car and went into the dining room. The attractive hostess seated Shelley where she could see the pool, leaving the menu beside her. The lunch hour crush was over, but the dining area was still comfortably full. The light reflecting from the pool and the pink, white and mauve color scheme of the room had a soothing effect on Shelley. Her light coral top and slightly deeper shade of coral jeans harmonized well with the decor. Her iridescent coral Reeboks were not only fun, the little that she allowed herself, but also had been easy to find, and easy to slip into as she was slipping away.

Waiting for her lunch to be brought, Shelley decided to order a sandwich to take with her. Open restaurants were rare in the Everglades, especially in April. While she was eating her shrimp and avocado salad and buttering a roll, new strategies started perking through her head. She couldn't afford the dangerous daydreaming that had nearly annihilated her.

After paying her check and putting her sandwich into the large soft leather pouch hanging from her shoulder, she made a point of stopping at the main desk on her way out. Although she had chosen the restaurant for its anonymity, her plans now included laying a false trail.

She asked for directions to Miami and for a map of that city. She burbled happily of how she had come from St. Petersburg and had gone down to the Keys for two days, "Much too short a time to see anything", and could the receptionist suggest a place to stay in Miami, perhaps even make a reservation for her in one of their chain of motels? The receptionist was quite accommodating, and Shelley left feeling hopeful, with a receipt for a hotel room she had no intention of using tucked safely in her bag—, a red herring to confuse her handsome tracker.

In a state of euphoria, Shelley drove across the bridge connecting Key Largo to the mainland of Florida. Thinking out loud again, she murmured, 'I'll go north at Florida City instead of northeast toward Miami. Dirk should be in Miami by now. His car can cover the miles much faster than mine."

She reached over and flicked on the radio for company. Humming along softly with Julio and glancing about at the green fields of truck farms, Shelley came back to reality with a thud. "Isn't that a Continental on the side of the road up there?" She slammed her fist against the dashboard. "It is, dammit, it is! Now what?" Too far to see the color in the glare of the sun, Shelley took her foot off the accelerator and coasted over onto the side of the road. Sitting there quietly watchful, she could see someone moving around the Continental. Not recognizing the silhouette, which was not as tall or as lean as she expected, she slowly shifted gears and pulled out on the highway. "Thank God," she noted as she approached the car, "It's dark blue, not the maroon I feared."

Just then the driver came around the back of the car, his shirt of brilliantly colored hibiscus blossoms stretched across an unhealthy paunch. Shelley started to giggle in relief, a relief that was short lived. How could she be so complacent? Dirk might not be in Miami. He must have figured out by now that he could have passed her. Then all he'd have to do is wait. Oh yes, that parked Continental was a warning. She'd be glad when she reached the Tamiami Trail, but she'd be much more watchful en route.

On the outskirts of Miami, the driver of the long maroon Continental swore softly to himself. He should have overtaken her by now. How could he have missed her? He pulled over to the side of the road and gazed unseeingly through his dark wraparound glasses. He shrugged out of his snuggly fitting brown jacket and tossed it onto the back seat. Loosening his tie, he unbuttoned his collar and stretched, his muscles rippling against the plush seat. He tranced again, seemingly unaware of his fingers beating a tattoo on the wheel. His musings were interrupted by the ringing of his car phone.

"Yes", he snapped into the mouthpiece.

"Mr. Gentile, we've located a reservation for tonight for a Shelley Morgan in a motel here in Miami. A Holiday Inn. Shall we send someone there to wait?"

"Good job, Banks. No. I'm in the area. I'll meet her myself."

Setting the phone down slowly, Dirk's eyes narrowed. Shelley was not a stupid woman. Surely she knew of the network he had access to. Why would she deliberately book a room under her own name in a national chain? One so easily checked by Telex.

Seemingly of its own volition, the powerful Continental had started moving along I 95 and was even now pulling off the exit ramp leading to the motel. O.K. He'd go to the motel. And he'd wait. But not too long.

Some of the tension left her as Shelley reached the Tamiami Trail and turned west. Plowed fields of truck farms gave way to grassy meadows of the swamps. The view was broken now and then by little islands of hardwood trees. The famed mangrove swamp, with its twisting, knee-like roots, was nowhere in sight.

Spotting a roadside picnic bench under a shady tree, Shelley pulled off the highway to stretch her cramped muscles. The quiet of the swamp and the soothing bird calls were interrupted only by the occasional swish of a passing car and the rustling of the grasses. Nibbling her sandwich, feeling truly safe, or as safe as she was going to be until she reached Orlando and home, Shelley took a few minutes to unwind. But the worries and frustrations of the past week would not allow her to relax. She sat staring into space, sandwich forgotten,—recalling the highly unusual events of the last six days:

Shelley Morgan paused outside Hugh Donovan's office and wondered how she got herself in these messes. Taking a deep breath and shaking her head, she reached for the doorknob. It was wrenched from her hand, pulling her off balance. Suddenly she found herself tightly clasped in muscular arms, leaning against a comfortable masculine chest, and staring into silver eyes that had warmth that heated her soul.

"I'm awfully sorry. Are you hurt?'—The voice poured over her like dark chocolate."

"No, no. I'm fine," Shelley protested, continuing to stare.

"I didn't know you were there," the rumbling voice continued as the strong arms gently released her. "I don't usually go charging through doors, and colliding with people."

"It's O.K. Really." Shelley was half listening to the conversation. She watched entranced as a tanned hand brushed black curls off an equally tanned forehead. Was this Mr. Donovan, the club owner? If so, he was much younger than she had expected. Taking in the broad shoulders, the casual clothes, and the seemingly tightly-leashed energy, she sighed to herself. No wonder her mother played so much bridge.

"Are you sure you're all right?" The silvery eyes were doing an inventory of their own. She was tall, but not too tall. Wearing heels, she barely came to his chin. The soft coral suit presented her slim figure and complimented the fairness of her hair and skin. The collision had loosened some wisps of ash blond hair. As his eyes traveled over them, she blushed. Lowering her eyes, she self-consciously tucked the hair back into the topknot on her head.

When she raised her hand, the tall stranger became aware he was holding her upper arms. Dropping his hands as Shelley murmured again that she was fine, he gave a slight nod and went through the door, closing it after him, but taking with him the memory of amber eyes, black fans of eyelashes, and a haunting scent.

While the young receptionist continued to gaze wistfully at the closed door, Shelley gave her clothes a twitch, brushing the collision from her mind, clenched hands giving evidence of her concern about her meeting with Hugh Donovan as she walked toward the desk.

The receptionist, one ear encased in several pierced rings, turned toward Shelley and asked, "Yes? May I help you?" Her long purple fingernails remained poised over her keyboard.

"That wasn't Mr. Donovan, was it?"

"No such luck," the girl answered dreamily.

Shelley sighed with relief. Taking a deep breath, she continued, "My name is Shelley Morgan and I would like to see Mr. Donovan, please."

"Do you have an appointment?" the girl asked briskly, without checking the appointment diary lying open on the desk beside her.

"No, but—"

"Sorry. Mr. Donovan sees no one without an appointment." She turned firmly back to her computer.

Shelley persisted. "Will you check with Mr. Donovan, please? This is a personal matter concerning my mother, Kate Wilson. If you call his office, I am sure he *will* see me."

When the receptionist reached for the telephone, Shelley gave herself a pep talk. This is no time for nervousness. Act like you know Mr. Donovan will see you. Relax. Maybe you'll fool his receptionist, too.

Carrying on her inner conversation, Shelley walked over to look out the window. Below her some of Orlando's myriad lakes glittered like gems in the sun. Raising her eyes, she could imagine seeing the lift-offs at Cape Canaveral, many miles away.

She brushed a fleck of lint from her sleeve and caught the movement reflected in the window. She had been working at home when her mother called her in such distress, but had taken the time to twist up her hair, put on a little make-up, and get into her suit. She was counting on her business-like appearance to convince Mr. Donovan of the seriousness of her visit.

The receptionist put the phone down and said in a low, but carrying voice, "Miss Morgan, Mr. Donovan is busy now, but if you'll have a seat, he'll see you in about 15 minutes."

Shelley thanked her and walked over to sit on the comfortable loveseat. There were no magazines on the large coffee table. Evidently no one did see the man without an appointment.

Her feelings were quite jumbled and she still did not know exactly what she was going to say to Mr. Donovan when she finally saw him. She appreciated the time to try and organize her thoughts.

She didn't know what had gotten into her mother, pledging jewelry belonging to Frank as security for a debt. Those priceless jewels were museum quality and had been in his family over four hundred years. He was justly proud of the necklaces and had taken Kate and Shelley to the bank to show them off shortly after Kate and he were married. And Kate had borrowed one! Now she was having second thoughts and wanted it back.

Honestly! What kids did for their parents! But she owed her mother a lot. Things had been tough when her father died. She and her mother had grown closer, clinging to each other. Shelley shook her head. She'd really given Kate some problems. This is the least she could do.

The promised 15 minutes had stretched into a half-hour. There was still nothing to read. Thinking was just making her more stressed. Shelley stood to begin a walk to the window again just as the telephone on the receptionist's desk buzzed.

Putting the phone down, she said, "Mr. Donovan's Administrative Assistant is on her way, Miss Morgan. She'll take you to him.

Shelley nodded. "Thank you.

A well-dressed blonde, slim, tanned, and capable-looking, entered and smiled at Shelley. "If you'll come this way, Miss Morgan."

Shelley's heart was in her throat as she followed the Admin down the corridor. The young woman opened a door into a corner office, introduced Shelley, and withdrew. Shelley drew a deep breath before raising her eyes to meet Hugh Donovan's.

A tall, white-haired man stood behind the desk. He raised one eyebrow, "Miss Morgan? Kate Wilson's daughter? This is a surprise." He gestured toward a chair by the corner of the desk. "Won't you sit down?"

Shelley nodded and sank into the chair. An anxious glance around gave her an impression of plush upholstery and rich wood.

"How can I help you?" Hugh Donovan asked after resuming his seat.

Shelley shifted nervously and cleared her throat. "Kate Wilson is my mother.

"Yes."

Shelley began, "I really don't know how to say this, or even what to say."

Hugh studied her face. "Is it about your mother's debt?"

Shelley's eyes flashed to his. "Yes. Yes, it is," she said. Her voice was tinged with gratitude. "I've come to ask for the necklace back."

"I'm afraid I can't help you with that now," he said.

"Can't help me? But my mother gave you the necklace." Shelley sprang to her feet. "She's got to get it back. Please permit us to make some other arrangements to secure the debt," she pleaded.

"Miss Morgan, your mother gave me a very valuable necklace. I didn't realize it when she handed it to me, but it appears to be extremely old, and much too valuable to be here in my office. When I realized what I had, I called my attorney. I didn't want to be responsible for that necklace so I gave it to him for safekeeping." He stared at Shelley while he tapped his fingers on the desk.

"I'll give you my lawyer's name and address. Contact him. He can act for me. Whatever he agrees to do will be fine with me."

Shelley's heart lightened. With that endorsement, she was sure she could convince his lawyer to return the necklace and make other arrangements.

"Here's his card. His office is in the Flagler Square complex in Miami," Mr. Donovan said as he handed her the card.

Shelley looked at him in amazement. It was Friday noon. How could she get to Miami before the office closed! And how did the lawyer have the necklace so soon?

As if reading her mind, Donovan said, "Dirk has his own plane. He flew into Orlando Executive Airport this morning. He knew how worried I was."

If he was so worried, why hadn't he given it back to my mother, Shelley thought to herself. Aloud she said, "Thank you, Mr. Donovan, for agreeing to let Mr . . . . ah . . . ," she referred to the card, "Mr. Gentile act for you. And thank you for his card. I'm headed for Miami right away."

"That's 'Gen-teel', little lady. Rhymes with steel. That's what Dirk always says," he smiled. "And it's no problem. See what he can do." Looking Shelley over from head to toe, he chuckled. "Kate's daughter, eh? I'm surprised she'd admit it. You look more her sister. True, a younger sister, but still her sister."

Shelley nodded coolly while shaking his hand. Let him save that one for Kate. She had more important things on her mind. Leaving the elevator, Shelley looked for a telephone. She had to explain to Kate why she was leaving for Miami immediately. Cutting the phone call short when her mother's gratitude threatened to overwhelm her, Shelley headed for her car and the Florida Turnpike.

Tucking her toll ticket over the sun visor, Shelley started toward Miami. There was little traffic and she made marvelous time. Rob, her boyfriend, would have called her driving, 'flying low'. She gave her little red Cabriolet a loving pat on the dashboard and crooned to it, "Good girl, you're doing just fine. You'll get me there on time. I know you will."

Through the breaks in the scenic moss-draped woods, she could see very few houses. Now and again she passed open range, dotted with cattle. She could see citrus groves in the distance, the trees bright with fruit.

After driving through partially wooded areas and passing huge vegetable truck gardens, Shelley was delighted to reach West Palm Beach by ten minutes of three. Only 78 miles to Miami. That ought to be less than an hour and a half. She would get there well before the office closed.

The monotony of turnpike driving allowed her thoughts to drift back to her mother's disturbing visit that morning. It sounded as if her scatty mom had really done it this time. Shelley was sure her stepfather would never leave her mother, despite what Kate believed. Frank was very patient with his new wife. He might even enjoy being married to a kooky woman, especially one as attractive as Kate.

Recalling her mother saying she'd done some wild things in her life, Shelley's eyes widened in disbelief. That was the understatement of the year! Why, she could remember . . . . Well, that wasn't pertinent now; helping her mother was.

The traffic was heavier on the last stretch of the Turnpike and only allowed quick glances toward the tall hotels of the winter resorts. With a lighter heart, Shelley left the Turnpike near Pompano Beach and cut over to I-95 for a clear shot into Miami.

Traffic had already started getting heavier when one of Miami's brief afternoon showers caused the traffic to clog further. Reaching the exit ramp she needed, Shelley found it miraculously clear, paid her toll, and the little red car zipped through. Fortunately, the Flagler complex was on a direct route from the exit and there was parking under the building.

Even so, it was 4:50 pm when Shelley burst open the office door of Morris, Downs, and Gentile. The receptionist looked up cautiously from covering her computer.

"Please," Shelley said, hand extended. "I need to see Mr. Gentile right away."

"I'm sorry. Mr. Gentile isn't here," the motherly-looking receptionist said.

"Oh, no," Shelley said, shoulders drooping. "I really must see him. I've come all the way from Orlando."

"Mr. Gentile did have an appointment in Orlando this morning, but I think he flew from there to his home in Key West."

"Mr. Gentile lives in Key West?" Shelley asked in an unbelieving voice.

"No," the receptionist said with a smile. "He lives here in Miami. But his family has a home on Key West. He's gone there to spend the weekend."

Shelley tiredly pushed a strand of hair off her face. She hadn't eaten lunch. Her head ached. She hadn't even taken the time to freshen her lipstick. She must look a mess. Well, that was tough!

Raising her head and straightening her shoulders, she asked, "How far is it to Key West? You see, I have to talk to Mr. Gentile."

The receptionist nodded sympathetically. "About four hours," she said. "After you get out of Miami, that is. Miami is like any city on Friday night, almost total gridlock." She looked kindly at Shelley. "You'd be wise to stop and get a bite to eat and a cup of coffee." She waved her hand in the air. "Let the traffic clear up without you in it. You'll be just as far ahead and you'll have had a nice break, too."

".Thank you," Shelley said, turning away. The woman's kindness combined with her own lightheadedness almost brought tears to her eyes.

"There's a coffee shop on the ground floor of this building that's open until six" the receptionist volunteered.

"Thanks again," Shelley nodded as she went out the door. Very good advice, she said to herself. She's right. I really do need a break.

CHAPTER TWO

TWO ASPIRIN, SOME COFFEE, AND a sandwich made a big difference in Shelley's outlook. The latest telephone call to her mother helped also. She tried to be as upbeat as possible, refusing to let any negative thoughts enter the conversation. Kate was reassured, but vowed she would not discuss her gambling problem with Frank until Shelley arrived with the necklace. "Time enough then," was how she put it.

It took another hour to reach Key Largo. By then the sun had set. The highway south from there traveled over bridges and causeways, connecting the islands. Some strips of island were so narrow the Atlantic and the Gulf of Mexico lapped the shores on either side of the highway, but all this was lost on Shelley. Other than an occasional gleam of headlights on water, she drove through a tunnel of darkness whose perimeter was the area staked out by her headlights.

It was just eleven when she reached Key West and pulled over to the side of the road. One didn't go calling on a person one wanted a favor from at eleven o'clock at night. She leaned her head on the wheel in exhaustion. She just could not negotiate the return of Frank's necklace tonight.

Regrouping was the better part of valor, Shelley decided, and checked into a small motel. She looked through the phone book for Dirk Gentile's telephone number and address. Writing both numbers on a slip of notepaper to have them ready for the morning, Shelley undressed and crept into bed, falling immediately into a deep sleep. True, she spent much of the night dreaming of chasing things and of driving along dark roads and crossing steep bridges.

Morning finally came and she felt better after having a shower and washing her hair. Thankful the wrinkles had fallen out of the coral suit she had carefully hung up, she pulled on the slightly damp underwear she had rinsed out the night before. Well, it couldn't be helped. With luck, she'd be on her way home shortly and she'd soak in the tub for hours.

She breakfasted in the restaurant next to the motel and about 9:00 o'clock called the Gentile telephone number. A lady with a heavy Spanish accent answered and, after much difficulty, called Mr. Gentile to the phone.

"Dirk Gentile," a deep voice stated.

Shelley shivered at the sound.

"Mr. Gentile, my name is Shelley Morgan. I spoke with Mr. Donovan yesterday. He gave you a package in Orlando and I would like to see you to discuss it."

"Miss Morgan, this is my day off," the voice reverberated over the telephone wire. "Talk to me now."

"I can't, Mr. Gentile. I must see you. Mr. Donovan suggested I see you." That was a slight misstatement. He had said 'talk', but how could she get the necklace without seeing him?

The deep voice sighed. "All right, but I can't see you until after one o'clock."

"That's fine. One o'clock it is. I'll be there.", Shelley whispered huskily, hardly daring to breathe for fear he'd change his mind.

She gave a sigh of relief as she put the phone down. He'd see her. So far, so good! But . . . what to do for four hours? She could check out of the motel around noon. She should be on her way home shortly after two, with any luck at all. She shuddered again. Dirk Gentile sounded very forbidding. He probably was as old as Mr. Donovan . . . but at least Mr. Donovan had been understanding. Perhaps Mr. Gentile would be, too. Kate was counting on her to get the necklace back.

Shelley returned to the motel to look at the map of Key West she had found in her room. Finding the address on the map, she decided to cruise by the Gentile house and check it out.

24

She drove down into the town and was amazed at the variety of homes. Many of the big old houses reminded her of those she had seen along the New England seacoast. But the lush vegetation, the colorful hibiscus and magnificent bougainvillea, the brilliant birds darting and twittering, all proved these homes were in a tropical climate. Some houses appeared to be made of conch shell plaster, painted in pastel tones. The Ernest Hemingway home, sign prominently displayed, was an imposing Spanish colonial-style mansion. And everywhere there were palm trees and the evergreen of magnolias.

Giving herself a shake to break the spell of the charming town and its tiny shops, Shelley reminded herself she was here on business. Driving on south, she found her resolutions forgotten as she passed small wooden houses, also painted in pastels, with tiny porches, white picket fences tight against the sidewalks, and gardens a riot of flowers.

The Atlantic soon was sparkling before her. Turning to drive along the oceanfront highway, she came to the Gentile address. She stopped across the street in awe. It was one of the older homes, two stories high and influenced by Spanish architecture. The warm red tiles of the roof glowed in the sun. A high stone wall that looked as if it were made of chunks of coral surrounded the grounds. The house, hidden by the rich greenery of the garden, was barely visible through an ornate wrought-iron gate.

Dirk Gentile's family must have been here for generations, Shelley mused. No wonder he wanted to spend his weekends here. He'd only have to cross the road for a morning swim in that beautiful green ocean.

As she turned to admire the ocean, a swimmer splashed out of the water onto the deserted sands of the glistening beach. It was difficult to see him clearly, silhouetted as he was against the sparkling water, but Shelley got the impression that Mr. America could begin to worry about his crown. She squinted into the glare and watched his muscles ripple as he picked up a towel to rub at his curly black hair.

She saw him look at her little car. Hooking the towel purposefully around his neck, he started through the sand toward her. Shelley panicked, turned the key in the ignition, and zoomed away, leaving the man framed in the rearview mirror, staring after her.

She didn't know who he was, but she wasn't ready to meet any of the residents until one o'clock. Then she only wanted to talk to Dirk Gentile, convince him to return the necklace, and head for home.

One o'clock seemed a long time coming, but as it neared, Shelley started back toward Gentile's. Although Key West was the largest of the keys, it didn't take very long to get from one place to another. Naturally, she was there early. After fidgeting in the car for a few minutes, she decided to go to the door. If he would see her now, she could get an earlier start toward home. Heaven knows, it would be a long drive.

There was a bell pull in the pillar by the gate and Shelley gave it a hefty tug. She heard no sound and could only hope it gave a signal inside the house. Peering through the gate, she was delighted to see a small, dark-haired woman in a white uniform heading her way.

"Si?" the woman said in a questioning tone when she reached the gate.

Oh, yes. This must be the woman Shelley had talked with earlier. "Mr. Gentile, por favor? I'm Shelley Morgan," she said slowly. "I talked with you this morning.

"Ah, si! Si! Favor de entrar," the lady nodded with a gleaming smile, indicating that Shelley should enter. "Si. Señor Gentile."

Shelley nodded and smiled as she followed her down the crushed stone walk. Entering the cool darkness of the house, she was momentarily blinded after leaving the brilliant sunlight.

"Señor Gentile, he eat now," the woman said, gesturing to a bench in the entrance hall. "Aqui, por favor."

Shelley sank onto the bench gratefully, as the woman hurried down the long corridor. She had not decided how to approach Dirk Gentile. Mulling her thoughts over in her mind, she looked around. The floor was earth-toned tile. A heavy, dark wooden staircase rose to the second floor. An elaborately carved Spanish chest stood along the wall with a large mirror framed in dark wood hanging above it.

The house was cool and fragrant. Fragrant? Yes, fragrant, the scent of a pomander ball, orange overlaid with cloves. It was a scent that brought back memories of Christmases past, and of her Dad.

A door opened farther along the hall. The sun streaming through the sliding glass doors at the end of the corridor outlined the silhouette of a large man approaching. There was something familiar about that silhouette but the man's compelling presence drove it from Shelley's mind. She rose to her feet in self-defense as he neared her. The dreaded meeting was due to begin.

"Miss Morgan?" asked the deep-chocolate voice. "Please come into the study. We can talk there."

Shelley shivered, hair on her arms prickling. What was there about that voice? She'd had the same reaction when they had spoken over the phone that morning.

She preceded him meekly into a book-lined library. A huge mahogany desk dominated the view from the doorway. Dirk Gentile indicated a chair beside the desk for Shelley to sit in, walked behind the desk, and seated himself.

She raised her eyes as she sat down and met Dirk Gentile for the first time as 'Dirk Gentile'. It was the man from the collision in Mr. Donovan's doorway. My, he was handsome: dark hair, silver-gray eyes, deeply-tanned complexion, tremendous shoulders. With his red shirt and black fitted slacks, he looked more like a pirate than a lawyer, and a dangerous pirate at that. She shook her head. Best to get on with her errand.

Before she could state her case, Dirk smiled. "I see we meet again. A pleasant surprise."

Shelley groaned inwardly. He appeared to be the swimmer from the beach this morning, as well. She hoped he didn't recognize her. It had been ridiculous to dash away like a frightened teenager. Now she wished she had stayed. She would have liked to have met Dirk Gentile under different circumstances.

Dirk recognized her immediately as the woman from Hugh's office. Her hair had been released from the twist on her head and it now curled softly around her face. Her coral suit lent a touch of color to her pale complexion. He was disappointed she didn't seem to recognize him. Ever the cautious lawyer, Dirk decided to hear what she had to say before pursuing the way they had originally met. He liked what he saw. But he didn't smile.

"You wanted this interview, Miss Morgan," he stated.

"Yes. Thank you for seeing me on your day off. This concerns your client, Hugh Donovan, and the package you received from him yesterday morning."

He merely nodded, secure in his intimidating position behind the desk.

"It's very important that we work out some arrangement to allow me to take that package home with me," Shelley continued.

"Why?" The deep voice echoed through her bones again.

"Why? Because it contains something my mother gave as security for a debt. I need to get it back and Mr. Donovan said you could act for him. Whatever you decide to do will be all right with him."

"What I decide to do, Miss Morgan, will be what's best for my client. It might not be best for you."

Dirk Gentile had picked up a pencil. He now began to tap it on the desk in front of him. Silver eyes narrowing, he said, "I've had no communication from Mr. Donovan since I left him yesterday morning. I'd need to hear this from him." He tossed the pencil on the desk. 'I don't know you. How do I know you are who you say you are?"

"I have my driver's license," began Shelley.

"Pah! What does that prove? Licenses can be forged." He swiveled in his chair and looked out the window, dark eyebrows lowered in thought. He stood abruptly, saying, "Excuse me," stalked out of the room and closed the door behind him.

Shelley was breathless. She'd found out he was not as old as Mr. Donahue and he was compellingly attractive. However, she felt as if she had been on the witness stand for hours.

He must be even more intimidating in the courtroom. Mr. Donovan was lucky Dirk Gentile was on his side. Shelley wished he were on hers.

She passed the time by studying the room. There were two walls of bookcases. At one end of the room, two long windows reached to the ceiling. Large bushes almost covered them and were trying valiantly to keep the brilliant sunshine from pouring in. A softly colored rug covered the floor, stretching to a long library table, which was pushed against the wall under a mirror.

Was the necklace here? It couldn't be in the bank or a safe deposit box; the banks were closed when he got here. Or were they? What time had he flown in?

No, she knew it wasn't in a bank. She had a feeling it was somewhere in the library. She could sense it. In the movies, the safe was always behind a picture or some books on a shelf. She wondered if the Gentile's safe was concealed in the same manner. If the necklace were here, it would be great. It would certainly be handy to return it to her.

The opening of the door drew Shelley's attention. Dirk stalked back in. "I can't reach Hugh to confirm your story. The butler at his home tells me he's gone away for the week-end." He stared sharply at Shelley. "Did you know that? Is that part of your scam?"

"Scam! What do you think I am, some two-bit thief such as you're used to dealing with? I came here to try to make some arrangements for the return of that package . . ."

"Package! Let's take the gloves off," Dirk interrupted. "I wouldn't have taken anything from Hugh unless I knew what it was. I didn't get where I am by not asking questions. I've seen the necklace! Now suppose you tell me what it has to do with you."

"Do you want the whole story?" ventured Shelley.

"Everything!"

"Well," Shelley began in a breathless voice, "Mr. Donovan owns the Myrtle Springs Club."

Dirk nodded.

"He has some rooms set aside for bridge games."

Again Dirk nodded.

"My mother is a good bridge player, of tournament caliber, but she's had a run of bad luck and has a debt she couldn't cover without asking her husband for the money. She doesn't want him to know how foolish she's been."

"Six thousand dollars," Dirk inserted.

"Six thousand dollars? Oh, my! Poor Mom. No wonder she's so upset.

"Go on," Dirk demanded. "How does the necklace enter into this? Hugh thinks it's very valuable, but it's so gaudy it looks fake."

"It's real," Shelley assured him. "It's an heirloom from my stepfather's family."

Dirk froze in his chair. Barely moving his lips, he said, "How did Mr. Donovan get it? I thought your mother didn't want your father, excuse me, your stepfather, to know about this."

"She doesn't. I mean, he doesn't. Know about the necklace, I mean."

"Who is your mother? Where is she? May I have her telephone number?"

"Do you want to call her now?"

"Yes," said Dirk emphatically.

"No. No, you can't," warned Shelley. "Her husband may be home."

"Why should that matter? Isn't the necklace his?" Dirk asked sharply.

"Well, yes. It is his," Shelley agreed slowly.

"Well, then?" Dirk, the lawyer, continued.

Shelley fidgeted in her chair. "You see . . . he doesn't know about this. My mother sort of borrowed it. That's why we must get it back and make other arrangements to pay off her debt."

Dirk leapt to his feet and leaned across the desk toward Shelley. "Borrowed it? Don't you mean stole it?" he said in a cold voice.

"No. No," Shelley protested. "She'd never do that."

"No? 'Steal' means 'to take from another without detection; any surreptitious taking of anything tangible or intangible'. This makes me an accessory. I could be holding stolen property. I might be the receiver of stolen goods." Dirk pounded his fist on the desk. "I could be disbarred!"

He took a turn around the room, running his fingers through his hair. "Do you know what all this means?"

Shelley shook her head.

"I'm a party to larceny. Grand larceny, at that! Good God, woman! What was your mother thinking?" he said as he threw himself back into his chair and glared at her.

Shelley leaped to her feet. She leaned over the desk toward Dirk Gentile. "She wasn't thinking of larceny! And certainly not grand larceny!" she shouted back. "She was foolish and afraid to tell her husband how foolish she'd been."

"Does that make her a criminal?" She slapped her hand on the desk. "Are you married? I bet your wife would never tell you if she got in trouble. You don't appear to have a sympathetic bone in your body. You're too intimidating. Anybody can make a mistake. I'm here because I'm trying to help my mother rectify a mistake. She borrowed a necklace from her husband. I thought when people married they shared things. Is my mother a criminal? Does this make me a criminal, too?"

"If they are as close as you say they are, how is it she didn't talk over her money problems with him?" Dirk asked. "As a matter of fact, I'm not married. But if I were, I'd hope my wife and I could discuss anything and everything."

"You're right. One would expect that, in a marriage as close as my mother and Frank have,' Shelley agreed. "But Frank travels a lot. He does top level trouble shooting for Martin Marietta. Mom gets lonesome and bored. Especially bored. A problem like this would be difficult to discuss during a long distance phone call." Shelley smiled timidly at Dirk. "Better Bridge than another man."

Dirk raised his eyebrows and shrugged. Picking up a pen, he leaned back in his chair. He rolled the pen between his fingers as he stared over Shelley's head. Throwing the pen onto the desk, he stood and paced to the window and back.

"You don't understand the seriousness of this." Dirk stood in front of Shelley. "Both Hugh Donovan and I may have received stolen property. Your stepfather could have us prosecuted."

"Good grief!" Shelley rolled her eyes at the ceiling. "What a tempest over something that should be so simple!" She extended her left hand and arm in Dirk's direction. "You want out? Fine. Give me the necklace! Now you'll no longer have stolen property and my mom can return it!"

Dirk again threw himself into the chair behind the desk. "You do have some unusual ways of thinking, Miss Morgan. Devious reasoning abilities!" He leaned forward dejectedly, hands dangling between his knees. "I can't give you the necklace. Hugh entrusted it to me. I need his O.K. to release it."

Shelley stood with her fists doubled on her hips. "You're going to have to make up your mind which way suits you best," she said. "You can keep it and feel guilty, or you can give it to me and feel guilty. You won't be guilty, but you'll probably feel guilty for letting go of something entrusted to your care. The simplest thing you could do," she said, taking her turn to pace around the room, "is to let me make other arrangements to guarantee payment of my mother's debt and give the necklace back to me. Mr. Donovan said that you could act for him. So . . . act."

"I can't release the necklace without talking to Hugh," Dirk said, shaking his head. He leaned back in the chair. "Are you staying here in Key West?" he asked.

"I was," Shelley said, haltingly. "I stayed in a motel last night, but I checked out this morning. I was hoping to be on my way back to Orlando by now."

Dirk scraped his fingers through his hair again. "Perhaps you'd better check back in. I can't do anything until I talk to Hugh."

"But he could be away this whole week," Shelley protested. "I work. I must get back."

Dirk got to his feet and combed his fingers through his hair yet again, black curls falling over his forehead. "I'm sorry, but that's it. You're free to make whatever decision you feel is right. I'm just telling you my position."

Shelley sank into the chair where she had been sitting earlier and stared at the carpet. She'd come all this way . . . . It was unbearable to think of leaving without the necklace.

She raised her eyes to Dirk's face. "Do you have the necklace with you?"

"Yes"

"I mean, is it here and not in the bank?" she prodded, eyes searching his face. She almost missed the involuntary flick of Dirk's eyes as he glanced almost imperceptibly at the wall of bookcases.

"Yes," he said, as stoically as before.

37

We'll, at least it's here, Shelley said to herself. If he can get in touch with Mr. Donovan, it wouldn't present a problem to let me have it quickly. "I'll check back into the motel," she said aloud. "I must call my mother anyway and bring her up to date." She extended her right hand to Dirk. "Thank you, I guess."

He came around the desk to grasp her hand in his warm one, placing his left hand on top. "You do realize there's nothing personal in this? This has been strictly the lawyer talking, trying to protect his client."

The warmth from Dirk's hand spread through Shelley's body. This man is the enemy, she warned herself. Not ten minutes ago he was shouting at her. Now there was even a warm look in his eyes. If he is an enemy, why did she suddenly feel as if she had made a friend?

Evidently Dirk felt the warmth, too, for he suddenly loosed her hand and walked over to open the door. "Call me when you get settled. I'll keep you informed of any progress locating Hugh."

He walked out to the car with her. Shelley didn't know which would have been worse: to be so vibrantly aware of him beside her, or to have felt his eyes on her as she walked self-consciously to the car, alone.

The small motel where Shelley had stayed the night before had no vacancies. She had to settle for one of the larger and more impersonal of the many motels on Key West. The room had the usual spare toothbrush and toothpaste, as well as the cream, shower cap, and shampoo, but Shelley was longing for a change of clothing.

Driving back into town, she browsed through some of the small boutiques. She picked up a sundress sprigged with violets, a change of underwear, a pair of sandals, and a thin, candy-striped nightie.

Later, feeling fortified by a shower and the clean, new clothing, Shelley sank down in the comfortable chair by the window to call her mother. Kate was very brusque with her, asking for her telephone number, and telling her she would call her back. Shelley was more understanding when her mother mentioned Frank was at home.

While she was waiting for her mother to return her call, Shelley's next phone call was to Dirk, telling him what motel she was in and giving him the room number.

Shelley had been on Dirk's mind since she'd left his home. Before he thought, he asked her to have dinner with him.

"Thank you," she said, equally surprised, "but I don't think that would be wise." Very unwise, she said to herself. It would be fraternizing with the enemy. She had been daydreaming of seeing him coming from the ocean, remembering the magnificent build, the dark curls shining with ocean water, the powerful muscles . . . No, he'd just cause her to have disturbing thoughts. She'd only spend more time thinking about him.

Dirk was more piqued than relieved at Shelley's refusal, although the invitation had been issued without premeditation, completely out of character for him. He even thought twice about which shirt to wear.

"Perhaps you're right," he agreed. "I'll be in touch as soon as I reach Hugh, if not before."

In a few minutes the phone rang in Shelley's room. It was Kate, calling from the public phone at the 7-11 on the corner of her street. The phone was outside the store, so occasionally traffic noises interfered with their conversation. Kate was disappointed that the necklace had not yet been recovered. Shelley found it difficult to explain the delay without going into Dirk Gentile's threatening interpretation of Kate's having borrowed the heirloom necklace. Heaven knew Kate was upset enough as it was. Assuring her mother it was just a matter of the lawyer checking with Mr. Donovan, she left Kate feeling more optimistic than before.

The sun was beginning to set and, though it was dinner time, Shelley wasn't particularly hungry. She decided to get a sandwich and coke from the vending machine and take them out by the pool. It was very pleasant to sit in the gathering darkness, the soft evening winds rustling through palm trees and gently lifting Shelley's long blonde hair. Red strands of clouds were fading to a soft mauve, and sea gulls were making a last lazy wheel in the sky before heading for their nests.

She was remembering the events of the last two days. Was it really only two days? it felt like a week. Everything seemed to blur together. The one thing that stood out was how upset Dirk Gentile had been about getting and keeping the necklace. Stolen property, indeed! It was all in the family. At least that was what Kate and she believed. But Dirk . . . ! Wow! He was really worried. Could he truly be disbarred?

The perfect solution to all of this was for him to give her the necklace and have her sign a promissory note; then they could all get on with their lives. Dirk surely didn't sound very comfortable with keeping it. Shelley knew he'd feel much better when he got rid of it.

Slowly she straightened in the lounge chair. That was it! A half-formed idea had flitted through her head, and her brain reached out and grabbed it. All Shelley had to do was go to Dirk's and take the necklace back!

It was so simple! The more she thought about it, the surer she became that regaining the necklace would be best for everyone. Dirk wouldn't be disbarred. Neither Hugh Donovan nor Dirk Gentile could be prosecuted by Frank for receiving his 'borrowed' necklace. Kate would get the necklace back. She could give Mr. Donovan a promissory note, or borrow the money, or for that matter get it from Frank, once she replaced the necklace in the safe deposit box. Best of all, she, Shelley, could go home to Orlando.

Yes, she thought with mounting excitement. What a beautiful solution! Everybody would be happy. And she was positive the necklace was in Dirk's study. She'd seen his eyes flick toward that painting. She'd bet anything there was a safe or something behind it. She almost clapped her hands in delight!

The problem would be the combination for the safe. On TV people usually had the combination hidden in the desk. Dirk didn't look that gullible. Maybe he'd leave it in code somewhere around the room. She was feeling more hopeful again. With her background in computers and such, breaking a code would be a snap.

She would try it tonight. Dirk surely thought she was settled safely here in the motel. He'd never expect anything. And certainly not from her. She'd gotten the idea he didn't think much of her reasoning processes.

She'd need a flashlight, and had one in the car. She wished she had a set of picks or whatever it was they used to unhook doors, like Laura Holt or Remington Steele. She'd park her car down the street and walk up quietly. But she'd have to wait until quite late, probably three o'clock in the morning. That's when people should be sleeping most soundly. Shelley had read that somewhere, or maybe she'd heard it on TV in some detective story or other.

She didn't have an alarm clock, and she certainly wasn't going to ask the desk clerk to wake her at two in the morning. There was nothing for her to do but stay awake. She was too excited to think of sleeping anyhow. She could pick up a book at the news stand, and there was always television.

But Shelley couldn't settle herself to watch TV. Even reading didn't hold her attention. She found herself walking around the motel room, going from the bed to the dresser, over to the window, back to the dresser, picking up her purse, putting it down, picking up the pamphlets on the desk, putting them down. Never had the time passed so slowly. Finally 2:45 arrived. Shelley wished she had some dark clothing, but her sundress would have to do. She closed the door quietly behind her and crept out to her car.

CHAPTER THREE

THE CAR STARTED QUIETLY AT the first try and Shelley was on her way. She had no thought of failure. She knew what she planned to do was the perfect solution for everyone concerned.

It was rather eerie, being the only car on the road, all the houses dark. The few street lights she passed were haloed in mist. Shelley felt like a female knight on a holy quest. Her little red Cabriolet should have a streaming banner with a coat of arms on it . . . Frank's coat of arms, probably. There should be trumpets blaring in the background.

For a moment the unearthly quiet and oppressive darkness dampened her spirits. She wished she had put the top up on her car. It was so open, she felt exposed and vulnerable. But on the other hand, if she felt alone she probably was. No one appeared to be awake other than her.

Following her plan, she drove past the Gentile's and parked several houses down the road. She locked her purse in the glove compartment, put the flashlight in one of the big pockets of her sundress, her keys in the other, and started back up the road. The crunchy sand along the shoulder of the road was noisy and got in her sandals. After emptying her shoes for the second time, she moved over onto the grass. Much smoother! Much quieter!

Of course the huge wrought iron gate was locked. What had she expected? At least the house was dark. She walked around the high white wall and decided she had to go over it. Very gingerly she climbed up the stones. It was like climbing on sandpaper, but there were toe holds and places to put her fingers, so up she went. The wall seemed much higher when she was sitting on the top. The soft sounds of the ocean lapping the shore mingled with the gentle sound of the wind sighing through the trees, and over all she heard the imaginary trumpets sounding. Lady Shelley to the rescue! She shoved off from her perch and tumbled over as she landed.

Brushing herself off, she swept the area with a brief flash of the light to get her bearings. She tucked the flashlight back in her pocket, heading for the rear of the house. En route, she tried several of the windows. All were locked. Continuing on, she had the marvelous luck to find an unlocked door leading off the patio, directly into the "Florida Room" . . . that screened outdoor room, wicker furnished, lavishly cushioned, where people in Florida do most of their living.

French doors, leading into the house, were standing invitingly ajar. Shelley soon found the central hall and drifted like a shadow down to the door of the library. Standing quietly, she listened. Her own breathing and the normal night sounds of a sleeping house were all she heard.

However . . . all was not as it appeared. While Shelley was creeping through the house, a flashing light had been set off in Dirk's bedroom, waking him. The same heat sensor that triggered that alarm also alerted police headquarters, and a police car was dispatched to Gentile's.

Shelley opened the door to the library, unaware that her body's heat had betrayed her. She slipped inside, closing the door gently behind her. Giving the room a quick sweep with the flashlight, she returned it to her pocket and headed for the wall of bookcases. Enough light came through the windows to allow her to avoid the furniture.

Dirk shut off the alarm and waited by the window until he saw two policemen reach the gate. He inched down the stairs, pressed the signal to open the gate, then let them in through the front door.

When Shelley reached the bookcases, she felt her way along to where the painting hung. She tried to open it like a door, first off to the left, then to the right, but each time it swung back into place. Finally she tried lifting it off. That worked, so she turned and set it gently on the floor, leaning it against the desk. She turned back to the safe, but the clumsy flashlight in her pocket swung around, hitting a chair. Shelley froze. She stood there barely breathing, heart pounding, pulse racing . . . waiting. Hearing nothing, she turned back to the wall.

The police and Dirk were searching the ground floor, room by room, when they heard a noise come from the direction of the library. They stood quietly, waiting.

Shelley reached up to run her hand over the space that had been behind the painting. Nothing! A smooth blank wall was all she felt. She'd been so sure! As she reached into her pocket for the flashlight, the door burst open, the lights blazed on, and a voice shouted, "Freeze! Police!'

Shelley froze! Not even turning her head to see who was behind her.

"Turn around. Slowly," the voice continued.

She turned slowly, raising her arms, flashlight still in her hand, eyes blinking in protest at the bright lights.

"Holy cats!" said a rich southern drawl "Ef it ain't a girl!"

Shelley saw two policemen: one pointing a pistol, held in both hands, legs spread, ready for action; the older one had his thumbs tucked in his belt, a big grin on his face. She could see Dirk over the latter's shoulder. Walking in, he stopped just inside the door. He was barefoot and clad in a short maroon robe.

"What are you doing here, Miss Morgan?" he asked in astonishment.

Shelley only stared at him.

The policeman at the ready relaxed enough to stand straight, and held the pistol in only one hand.

The heavy-set policeman searched Dirk's face. "You know her, boy? What's yore daddy gonna say when ah tell him you got women breakin' inta the house after yew?" he chuckled. "Henry", he said to the young officer, "See if Miss Morgan's ahmed. Second thought, maybe ah'd better."

"That's not necessary," Dirk broke in. "I'm sure she's not armed."

"Are you, Miss?" asked the young policeman.

"Oh, no," said Shelley, in a low voice.

"We'll have to take you into the station, ma'am. 'Breaking and Entering' is mighty serious. Even to get at Dirk," the older policeman said.

Shelley shot a horrified look at Dirk, face white as sheet.

"Might get twenty years or so," he laughed, slapping his knee.

"Hollis, you're frightening Miss Morgan," Dirk warned.

"Shucks, boy, I can see you're just like yore daddy. He always had girls chasing after him when we was young. We stayed friends so long because I was happy to get his rejects."

"This might be a little more involved, Hollis," Dirk said.

"You want to press charges, Dirk Edward?" Hollis asked seriously. "That silent alarm works so good, she hasn't hardly had time to steal anything."

Again Shelley's wide eyes flashed to Dirk's face.

She looked so frightened, so vulnerable; he closed his eyes in anguish for her.

Hollis said, "It's all right to tease you, boy, and you may know her, but I have to see some ID."

"I have none here," Shelley said in a shaking voice. "My purse is locked in the glove compartment of my car."

"I didn't see a car when we pulled up," Henry said. "Where did you leave it, Miss?"

"I parked several houses down," she said in a low voice, "Sort of around the curve."

"Give Henry your keys, ma'am, and tell him what you're driving."

"A Volkswagen Cabriolet, an '85," she answered.

"You want to go with him or do you trust Henry to bring back your purse, intact?" Hollis asked her.

"Are they friends of yours?" she asked Dirk.

Dirk nodded. "Henry and I went to Key West High together. My dad and Hollis went to school together, too. They even served in the Navy together. Henry and I did our time in Vietnam."

Shelley listened, then nodded. "Yes, sir," she said to Hollis. "I'll trust him." She took the keys out of her pocket and handed them to Henry.

"While we're waiting for Henry, ma'am, I'm gonna have to read you your rights", Hollis said, looking at Shelley from under his grizzled eyebrows.

Shelley stared at him as if she were in a nightmare from which she could not waken as he rattled from "the right to remain silent" through "anything you say may be used against you in a court of law."

Somehow it had never sounded so damning on TV. For the first time, Shelley could appreciate Dirk's view of the whole situation.

"Now I'll ask you, ma'am," Hollis said, "Have you taken anything?"

"No," she said in a low voice.

"Were you looking for something in particular?"

Shelly looked at Dirk in panic.

"You don't have to answer that," Dirk said.

Hollis shot him an exasperated look.

"Dirk Edward, whose side are you on? You were about to get yourself robbed and now you're acting like the robber's lawyer." Hollis shook his head. "I don't understand you young fellas."

"All right, Missy. Let's try it another way. What were you looking for?" Hollis continued.

Again Shelley's eyes flashed to Dirk's face.

He shook his head imperceptibly.

Shelley stayed silent.

"Do you know Dirk Gentile?" Hollis asked, changing his tack.

"Yes," she said carefully, after checking with Dirk.

"How long have you known him?"

Again she looked at Dirk. He nodded slightly.

"I met him today. I mean Saturday."

"O.K.," Hollis said. "And when did you arrive in Key West?"

Again Dirk nodded.

"Friday evening. Late Friday evening," she replied.

"Now then, let's try it again. Were you looking for something in particular?"

Shelley remained silent, not needing Dirk's coaching this time.

In the silence, they heard the front door open and close. In a moment Henry appeared at the door of the study, Shelley's purse in his hand.

"Take out your ID, ma'am," Hollis said.

"Thank you," Shelley said to Henry as he handed her the keys and her purse. She reached in for her wallet, which she flipped open at her license.

It was Henry's turn to talk. "Take it out, please, ma'am."

She handed it to Henry. Hollis jerked his head toward the door. "Check it out with the station."

Henry disappeared.

"Any other ID, ma'am?" Hollis asked.

"Credit cards?" Shelley offered.

"No, ma'am. I was thinking more of a voter's registration card, or a passport."

"I don't have my passport," she said with dismay. "I don't carry that with me."

While she was flipping through the cards in her wallet, Henry returned.

"Neat as a pin," he said to Hollis. "Not a spot. Not even a traffic ticket."

Hollis nodded. "You want us to take her in, Dirk?"

"No," Dirk Gentile answered.

"Breakin' and enterin' with intent to commit a crime is an act the law classes as a felony. That's a mighty serious charge. We can't let her go scot-free. We should bring her up on charges."

"I didn't break in," Shelley inserted, some of her spunk coming back. "The door was unlocked."

Dirk noticed her color was better, too.

"All right," the officer said. "Forget the 'breakin' in'. You still 'entered'. If you didn't take anything, you were still trespassin'. That's only a misdemeanor. That's less serious than a felony, but we don't take kindly to trespassers here on Key West. Had too much trouble with those young'uns from up Miami way. Can't let you leave town 'til we check you out."

Dirk cleared his throat. "Uh, Hollis, I'll be responsible for Miss Morgan. After all, as far as we can see there's been no harm done."

"I don't know, Dirk Edward. Let me think on it a bit. I need her where I can get in touch with her if I need to."

"Would you consider releasing her into my custody?" Dirk asked.

"I might, you bein' a native son and all that. 'Course you bein' a lawyer don't hurt none." Hollis rubbed his jaw. "You bring her down to the judge Monday mornin'. We'll have it wrapped up legal."

Dirk looked and sounded as if that weren't too bad, but as far as Shelley was concerned, it was awful. The figurative banner she had started out with so gaily was not only dragging in the mud, it had been tromped on.

When Dirk returned from showing the policemen out, having thanked them for their prompt response to the alarm, Shelley was slumped in a chair. She looked up to thank him, only to see him looming over her like an avenging angel, silver eyes shooting sparks.

"All right, let's have it. What were you searching for?"

Shelley had learned her lesson well. She looked at him in stony silence.

Dirk hammered away, "Did you think the necklace was here?"

Again, no answer.

"Dammit, answer me! I didn't read you your rights. I'm not the police. Talk to me!"

Shelley just stared at him.

Dirk turned and paced, nervously running his fingers through his hair. Coming back to stand in front of her, he said conversationally, "You know, you are the most exasperating woman I've ever met. I'm trying to help you, but you just sit there and stare at me as if I'm some dangerous enemy."

Shelley shifted her stare to the corner of the room.

Dirk had evidently forgotten all he was wearing was his maroon robe, but Shelley hadn't. When he came over to lean down and put his hands on the arms of her chair, she could not refrain from staring at his muscular thighs. The top gaped open also, exposing the dark curls on his tanned and sinewy chest. Her hand almost reached out to touch him, imagining the warmth of his skin.

"Shelley," he pleaded. "Answer me. Were you looking for the necklace?"

"Yes," she whispered, mesmerized by the heat of his body and the maleness emanating from him.

"What made you think it was here?" he asked.

Shelley jerked her amber eyes to his face. "You said it was," she said breathlessly. "I asked you if it were here, and you said 'Yes'."

Dirk walked back to the bookcase and picked up the painting from the floor by the desk.

Shelley's breathing returned to normal.

"Did you think there was something behind this picture?" Dirk asked as he rehung it.

She nodded, keeping her eyes on the floor.

"A safe?" he asked.

Shelley nodded again.

"What made you think that?"

She raised her eyes and flicked them to the painting, now restored to the wall. "That's where it would be if this were TV or the movies."

"Ah, Shelley," Dirk sighed, "but this isn't TV. These are real jewels and these are real problems."

Shelley sniffed, lower lip trembling.

"Those were real policemen, as much as Hollis likes to ham it up. And it was a real lock-up he was talking about."

Shelley sniffed again and a fat tear rolled down her cheek.

"I don't mean to sound self-centered, but I make my living as a lawyer. I don't want to be disbarred. Besides which, it would kill my dad."

Shelley gave a soft sob and rubbed at her cheek.

Dirk stopped in front of her. Then he reached down and pulled her to her feet. He drew her head to his chest and held it there, patting her gently on the back with his other hand.

"I've heard the way you think." he said soothingly. "I know you didn't see this in terms of 'Breaking and entering with intent to steal', but the police do."

Shelley gave a wail, and burrowed into Dirk's chest, grabbing him tightly around the waist.

"It's O.K. I also believe you when you say neither your mother nor you thought of this in terms of larceny."

Shelley turned her head to lay her cheek on Dirk's warm chest, quieter but still sniffing. She couldn't think of anywhere she'd rather be than right here, the way she was.

Dirk's hands became restless. They roamed over her shoulders, her back, down her backbone, patting, petting . . . . He moved closer to her, hands still wandering.

Her sniffs quieted. Her hands were moving searchingly over the muscles that covered his ribs. They stood there, enjoying the warmth and the comforting for a few minutes, touch feathering lightly over each other. Dirk's breathing began to change, becoming deeper and faster. His hands strayed to just below Shelley's waist and back to her shoulders. They returned lower, drifting to the top of her hips. They brushed lightly up to the nape of her neck, where one soothed Shelley's tense muscles.

She was barely awake, so gentle was his touch, when seemingly without his volition, his hands made their lowest pass yet and pulled her snugly against his lower body. Shelley stiffened. What would Rob think? She pulled away with difficulty.

A sigh that was almost a groan proved that the temptation had been too much for him. He leaned his forehead against hers "I've been wanting to have you in my arms again since that first moment I saw you. And when I saw you, sitting in that little convertible, sunlight glinting on your hair, I could hardly believe my luck."

He had recognized her on the beach front. Why hadn't he mentioned that? She thought he'd been referring to the collision in Mr. Donovan's office. What kind of game was he playing?

His hands slid down her arms, clasping her hands in his. "I ran into you first Friday morning in Hugh's office. I literally knocked a woman off her feet. Can you imagine how disconcerting that can be to a man when said woman appears not to remember the encounter; an encounter that may change that man's life? Very ego deflating! I suppose I should be grateful you weren't planning to sue me," he laughed.

"Oh, no. I remember." Shelley sighed. "I was concerned whether you were Mr. Donovan or not. My meeting with him was worrying me. I was just glad to find out he was still in the office".

"Well, I remembered you," Dirk said huskily. "I had never seen amber eyes before."

Shelley flashed a look at him and then glanced away. "Yes. Well, ah . . . I think I'll leave now."

"Leave?" Dirk repeated dazedly. "Leave? You can't leave," he said in a stronger voice. "You have to stay here."

"I can't stay here. I have a motel room. My things are there. I must go back," Shelley protested.

"No," Dirk said firmly, running his fingers agitatedly through his hair again. "I mean you <u>may not</u> leave because you're in my custody."

"So . . . ?"

"This means you must stay here, with me."

"I will not! Uh-uh. No way!" Shelley said as she backed away, hands raised, palms outward.

"Shelley Morgan, contrary to what you might think after what just happened, I am not a white slaver, nor am I looking for a mistress! You heard Hollis." Dirk recalled the facts for her. "You were placed in my custody until this thing is settled. We must go to court about it Monday morning."

"I didn't think he meant that," Shelley said in a small voice.

"Like I said before," Dirk said in exasperation, "Hollis Johnson likes to ham it up. He plays like he's part of the 'good ol' boy' network, but he's sharp as can be and a good lawman. He and my dad went to Georgia Tech together. He ran his own corporation for years. It's only since he retired that he turned to police work on Key West. He's a conch, as I am, and he had no trouble getting on the force. If the town didn't pay his salary, I think he'd pay them," he said disgustedly.

"Conch? What's a conch?" asked Shelley.

"A native of Key West," Dirk saw. "People born here. I guess it's because we eat so much conch chowder and fried conch."

Dirk whirled to confront her, face red, hands on hips, causing the maroon robe to gap dangerously. "You did it again! You changed the subject. To get back to it: you're in my custody. You stay with me until this is straightened out."

"Stay with you?" whispered Shelley.

"In my home."

"In your home?" she repeated.

"You'll be my guest. Nuncie will love fussing over you."

"Nuncie?"

"Annunciata Jueves. The maid. You met her when you were here earlier."

"Oh. Oh, yes," she said, happy not to be repeating.

Looking beyond his shoulder, she could see a pale pink glow in the sky. Dawn was breaking and the birds were beginning to chirp sleepily in the trees.

"It's morning," she said in astonishment.

"We may as well get your things from the motel, now. When you're settled in, you can sleep for a few hours and then we'll have brunch. Let me get dressed. I'll be right back." He started for the door, then turned. "Don't try to leave!" he said ominously.

Shelley shook her head and looked at him from under her eyebrows. "I won't."

They parked the little Cabriolet on the driveway inside the white stone wall before Dirk drove Shelley to the motel in his Lincoln. When he started to go into the room with her, she blocked the door. "No," she said firmly. 'I'm in your custody. I won't run off. What I have to pack won't take two minutes. You can wait in the car or meet me at the desk when I check out, but we don't have to be Siamese twins."

Dirk stared at her intently before nodding and turning toward the cashier's office.

Shelley was correct. It hadn't taken more than two minutes to put her unused nightie, her coral suit and heels, and the cosmetics from the room into one of the plastic bags her purchases had come in. She went into the office to settle the telephone charges and there was Dirk, leaning on the desk, talking to the night manager and calling him by his first name.

He must know everybody was her first thought. The second one was worse, and she blushed to think of it. The manager probably thought she had spent the night with Dirk Gentile. She blushed even brighter. Technically, it would be difficult to say she hadn't.

They returned to the house by way of the oceanfront highway, instead of through town. The noise of the small planes landing and taking off from the airport reminded Shelley of a hive of bees.

"Is your plane there?" she asked Dirk.

He looked at her in surprise. "Yes. Yes, it is," he smiled.

"You were leaving Mr. Donovan's office as I arrived. The lady in Miami said you flew directly here." She shrugged and gave a half smile. "Two and two," she said.

Nuncie was delighted to show her to a bedroom decorated in peach and aqua pastels. It was on the cool, shaded side of the house and Shelley was soon in her new nightie, sliding under the covers.

A tap on the door awakened her a little after noon. Dressing hurriedly, she dashed down the stairs. Nuncie led her into the Florida Room and seated her at the round table in the comer. A sheer tablecloth, lightly embroidered, white on white, covered the glass topped table, and with the colorful china and brilliantly-colored fruit, made a feast for the eyes.

Sparkling glasses of juice, tinkling with ice, were set beside the avocados filled with a conch salad. Accompanying these were fried, puffy balls of pastry, hinting of garlic and onions.

"Are these hush puppies?" Shelley asked Nuncie.

Nuncie shook her head and said, "Bollos," rattling off some Spanish as she passed them to Dirk.

"She says, 'Eat them while they're hot and crisp'. Haven't you had these before?" he asked.

Shelley shook her head, mouth being full of fragrant and tasty bollos.

"I thought they might be finding their way north", he said. "They're sold by the sackful at the outdoor stands in town, but we think Nuncie makes the best bollos in Key West."

He turned to Nuncie and repeated his compliment in Spanish.

She ducked her head and smiled, "Gracias, Señor Dirk."

Taking steaming cups of fragrant coffee over to the gaily cushioned wicker chairs when they had finished eating, they did what most Americans do on Sundays: they read the Sunday paper, in this case the Miami Herald.

Shelley grabbed the <u>Living Today</u> section to read her horoscope, which warned of trouble in following rules. She gave a black cursory look at the Bridge column. If it weren't for Bridge . . . .

There was a beautiful spread on the Symphony Showhouse, opening the next weekend. The house to be opened to the public was the winter home of a former ambassador, and the photographs in the article promised an event that would keep the Symphony solvent for another year.

She glanced up from the <u>Tropic</u> magazine section. "Do you read 'Person To Person'?" she asked Dirk. At the shake of his head, she said, "Some of these personals are really off the wall.

But some break your heart. There are so many lonely people out there." She was quiet for a minute. Then she continued, as if to herself, "That's my mom's problem. She loves Frank and he adores her, but he's so busy. She gets so lonesome when he's away."

Dirk looked up from the crossword puzzle he was working. "No doubt that's how she got so involved in bridge games. What does your stepfather do?"

"He's retired from the Air Force, a Colonel. The area where they live is surrounded by aircraft industry and NASA installations. He became a consultant, a very busy one. He travels all over: Baltimore, Louisiana, Denver, California. He really doesn't need to work so hard."

"Perhaps some good will come out of this mess," Dirk mused. "They'll be forced to make some adjustments."

He tossed the puzzle and the pen he was using onto the coffee table and walked behind her chair. He put his hands on her shoulders, left bare by the thin straps of her sundress. Absent-mindedly he caressed them. "Let's go swimming," he suggested.

"But I don't have a suit," Shelley protested. "I didn't bring any clothes with me. I never expected to be here this long."

"Oh, right! Let's go over to the Sheraton. Their boutiques are open Sundays. We'll pick one up for you."

"No, 'We' won't. 'I' will. I'll get what I need. It's enough I'm a guest here."

"Ah, but you wouldn't be my guest if you weren't in my custody," Dirk said slyly.

"True. But if I hadn't been caught, I'd be home by now."

"O.K. It's a draw," laughed Dirk. "We'll cross each bridge as we come to it."

Somehow that statement didn't set Shelley's heart at ease.

CHAPTER FOUR

THE TIDE WAS RECEDING AND the murmur of the waves blended with the rustle of the palm trees overhead. Shelley was drowsing on the blanket Dirk had spread on the brilliant sand, the April sun warm against her back. Dirk was sitting, his back against a palm tree, watching Shelley bask in the sun. His eyes danced as he began to whistle softly. Shelley lifted her head toward him as the melody of "Itsy, Bitsy, Teeny, Weenie, Yellow Polka Dot Bikini" penetrated her somnolent state.

"You're late with your complaining. You should have protested when you saw me buying this suit."

"Who's complaining? Not me!"

"What's your problem then?" Shelley said, pulling her arms up to rest on her elbows. "You don't like yellow? . . . or polka dots? . . . or is something else bothering you?"

"Oh, yeah," he grinned. "Something else is bothering me. But we won't go into that right now." He paused a moment. "I thought you might like me to put some sun lotion on your back. You're getting a little pink."

"Thanks. That would be nice," Shelley said, sitting up. "We don't have as much sun in Orlando as you do. We seem to have a lot more rain, especially in late winter and early spring. And the sun is a lot warmer here. You wouldn't think 400 miles would make such a difference."

Dirk knelt behind her while she unselfconsciously loosened the halter strap on her bikini top. He groaned to himself as he gently smoothed the lotion over Shelley's silky shoulders and back. No mere mortal should have to be exposed to this, he sighed. He was shocked to hear himself saying, "Lie down on your stomach. I'll do the backs of your legs, too."

Shelley was not unmoved, either. She had noticed his powerful shoulders, and she could almost feel her hands smoothing over those wonderful muscles in his arms. He had a narrow waist and a taut abdomen that called attention to the red strip of bathing suit he was wearing. Somehow the heat she felt was not all from the sun. Dirk's masculine hands had added their share of the heat.

"No. No, thanks," she breathed. "I can do the rest. Thank you for doing my back."

"No problem." Dirk moved back to lean against the palm tree. No problem? Who was he kidding! Dirk rolled his eyes and took a deep breath. Would it have been better for him to put the lotion on Shelley or was it worse to watch her smooth it over her satiny skin?

Dirk cleared his throat. "Do you date anyone seriously?"

"Yes. I have a boyfriend, Rob. We've been dating about a year or so." On another level Shelley was appalled. Dear, sweet, blue-eyed Rob. She hadn't given him a thought since she'd left Orlando. She 'tsked' at herself, and then asked politely, "How about you? Are you involved?" She wondered why the answer mattered to her. No man as handsome as Dirk could be roaming around off-leash.

"There's a junior partner I've been dating." Shelley's heart sank. "But we're not too involved. She's ambitious and serious about her career. I wouldn't be surprised to see her make D.A. in a few more years."

Shelley breathed more easily and then felt guilty about it. While she was reacting to this, she realized Dirk was asking, "What do you do?"

"I'm Technical Editor for *P. C. Universal*, a computer magazine based in Tallahassee. It has great U.S. circulation, and there's talk of us going international.

"Tallahassee? I thought you were from Orlando?"

"I am," Shelley agreed. "I work at home. I connect into the network in 'Big T' which works out fine. Of course, Mom

69

always knows how to get in touch with me." For a brief moment she and Dirk stared at each other, reminded of why Shelley was there. Giving herself a mental shake, she continued, "It doesn't matter where I test the new equipment or the new software, as long as my reviews get to the magazine in time to make my deadline."

"Un-huh," Dirk agreed distractedly. "Ah . . . how about you and Rob? A year's dating sounds serious. Are you?"

"No," Shelley answered slowly. "Rob's vice-president of a nationally-connected travel agency, so he travels quite a bit, both in the U. S. and abroad. When he's home, we date. When he's away, we don't." She shrugged. "I'm not dating anyone else right now."

Dirk smiled complacently. Now why should that news have made him feel like smiling, he wondered.

Shelley sat staring at the waves rippling on the shore and then looked up and down the beach. "This is practically a private beach. There's no one else around. Are there 'No Trespassing' signs posted?"

"No," Dirk laughed. "It's just that few people use it this time of year. Mostly Northerners. As warm as it seems to you, it's cool for the Conchs, especially now the sun is getting lower. The palms are starting to shade the sand."

Shelley nodded in agreement, then she said, "Are there many shells left on the beach? Could we walk along and look for some?"

Dirk had risen at her questions, and now reached down for her hand. Shelley had started to gather her lotion and the blanket and towels.

"Leave them," Dirk said with a shrug. "As you said, there's nobody around."

They walked toward the water's edge, Shelley's hand nestled securely in Dirk's. No one seemed eager to break the connection.

After the walk up the beach, Shelley returned jubilantly with a perfectly formed conch shell cradled in her arms. The peach outer shell was beautiful, but it merely enhanced the pearly inner lining.

"Oh, Dirk. Isn't it beautiful?" Shelley gazed at him, her eyes like stars. "And weren't we fortunate to find it?" She practically danced with excitement.

Dirk found himself with his arm around Shelley's shoulders. What was there about this woman? He couldn't keep his hands off her.

He turned her to face him, hands at her shoulders, his eyes, smoky with desire, roaming over her face. "Yes, it is beautiful," he agreed. Turning away abruptly, he began to gather the towels and blanket. "And we were even luckier no one was living in it," he teased. "I can picture you heaving it out to sea the moment the poor conch stuck his head out . . . or his foot, whichever."

"I wouldn't do that," Shelley protested.

"No?" Dirk's left eyebrow rose to express his disbelief.

"Well, maybe," Shelley giggled. "It would have been rather a surprise."

Turning to cross the road to the house, blanket and towels tucked under one arm and Shelley tucked under the other, Dirk decided he was a happy man.

The next morning Shelley, dressed in her coral suit, was at the breakfast table by eight o'clock. The flowers were vibrant, and the sun streaming into the room almost made her forget their appointment with the judge that morning. Nuncie met her at the door of the Florida room and led her to a chair, wide smile on her face, apron covering her generous form. She clucked over Shelley, murmuring in Spanish that she was pale and thin, and urging her to have more of everything to eat.

Shelley was growing more and more impatient as the time passed.

"What time does Mr. Gentile usually have breakfast?" she asked.

"Soon. Soon," Nuncie said, disappearing into the kitchen for more coffee.

Just before nine Dirk appeared, dressed in jeans, T-shirt, and disreputable running shoes, yawning, and begging for coffee.

Shelley stared at him in amazement. "Why aren't you dressed?" she demanded.

Dirk looked down at his T-shirt and then back at Shelley. "I am," he said.

"Are you planning to see the judge looking like that?" Shelley asked in a horrified tone.

Nuncie set a mug of steaming coffee in front of Dirk. Cradling it in his hands, he raised it to his lips and took several grateful sips.

"No judge," he mumbled.

"No judge?" Shelley exclaimed. "What do you mean, 'No judge'? Today is Monday. We have to appear before the judge on Monday."

Dirk shook his head. "Discoverer's Day".

"Discoverer's Day! Oh, no." Shelley groaned. "Discoverer's Day. No courts?"

"No courts."

"I'll have to stay another day?"

"You'll have to stay."

"I can't stay. I just can't stay." Shelley leapt to her feet and paced around the room. "May I use your phone? I'll have to call the office to arrange for some time off."

Dirk waved toward the study. "Go ahead."

By the time Shelley returned, Dirk was coming to life. "What happened?"

"No answer. The office must be closed." Shelley raised her eyes to the ceiling. "I can't believe I forgot this holiday. She sat down heavily at the table.

Dirk was sympathetic. "It was easy. You had a lot on your mind. You're far from home. You're tired. Lots of reasons."

"I don't know if that makes me feel better or not," Shelley laughed shakily.

Veering off on a tangent, she continued, "Maybe the club is open. Perhaps Mr. Donovan's there and you can discuss the necklace with him."

Dirk stared at her. "I'll give you 'A' for persistence." Setting the mug on the table, he rose to his feet. "Mas cafe, Nuncie, por favor," he said as he left the room.

Before Nuncie could pour the coffee, he was back. "Club closed, too?" Shelley asked.

"No. The club is open. But since it's a holiday, Hugh decided to extend his weekend."

Watching Dirk sit and drink his coffee, Shelley leaned her head on her hand, elbow on the table. "I feel as if I'm in a dream sequence in some experimental theatre play. Any moment I keep thinking I'll wake up."

Dirk put his head on the table, shoulders shaking. When he sat up, he wiped his eyes with his hand, and in a choking voice said, "Esther wouldn't believe this. She's never even seen me smile before ten o'clock, and as to seeing me laughing this early, well . . ."

"I didn't think my comment was all that amusing," Shelley said haughtily. "You evidently don't understand how frustrating this is for me. This holiday today is just one more obstacle."

"I didn't mean to hurt you, Shelley. I know how upset you must be. All things considered, I think you're taking this very well."

Nuncie bustled in to set a basket of hot biscuits on the table. She pushed the pats of butter and the jar of honey toward Dirk.

Watching the steam rise and the butter melting on the biscuit he had cut open, he said to Shelley, "Today would appear to be a wasted day as far as straightening out this necklace business. How would you like to go out on my boat with me? It's very peaceful on the water. We could drop a line over—fish a little, swim a little. What do you say?"

"I really want to get this settled, but you're right. There's nothing we can do today."

"Then we go!" Dirk put his arm around Shelley's waist and hugged her to him. Turning, with his arm still around her, he asked Nuncie to pack a lunch to take with them. "And not just tacos," he warned.

"Wear your bikini," he said, looking down at Shelley. "Do you have a jacket or a cover-up?"

"You know I don't. The only thing remotely resembling one is this silk blouse to my suit."

"Right! Wasn't thinking. I'll lend you one of my shirts. Go and get changed."

The low hum of the engine was the only sound competing with gulls mewing overhead. The sun reflected off the shining chrome and white of the bulkheads. The polished deck was warm underfoot. The cabin cruiser cut through the waves, ocean breezes tossing Shelley's long blonde hair into a tousled mass. She stood beside the cabin, fingers lightly touching the rail to hold her balance, Dirk's borrowed shirt fluttering around her thighs. The salt spray cooled her skin under the relentless sun.

With the cruiser on automatic pilot, Dirk turned to watch Shelley. From his view up on the flying bridge, he decided Shelley-watching could become his favorite occupation. She looked exhilarated, smiling into the wind, as if there were nowhere else she would rather be. And sexy as hell in his shirt! What possessed him to <u>offer</u> her his shirt? You're losin' it, man, he said to himself as he turned back to the controls.

Little could he know Shelley had a worry on her mind, too. *DOUBLE OR NOTHING*. What kind of name was that for a boat? Was Dirk more involved with Mr. Donovan's gambling club than he had led her to believe? It's what gamblers said all the time, wasn't it? 'Double or nothing.' At least they did in the few TV shows she'd seen.

"How far are we from Cuba?" she called up to Dirk, not taking her eyes from the marine hues of the water.

"About 90 miles. Why? Did you want to go there?"

"Heavens, no. I was just wondering." Mmph. That close. With a forty-foot cruiser like Dirk's, ninety miles would be nothing. He seemed to have a lot of money . . . a maid . . . two homes . . . his own plane . . . . But he was too straight arrow to be involved in drugs . . . or gun smuggling . . . wasn't he? Besides, he had policemen as friends. But on the other hand, gambling . . .

During Shelley's musings they had been approaching a small island. She looked over the side and was delighted to see shells on the white sand of the ocean floor beneath them. Several large fish swam lazily through a school of brilliant tropical fish which darted about, changing directions in a flash of colors.

"Aren't you afraid you'll scrape the bottom of the boat? It's so shallow here."

"The depth finder says it's about eleven fathoms deep. That's over sixty feet. I don't think I'd try to wade ashore if I were you."

"Sixty feet," Shelley echoed. "I can see shells lying on the bottom," she said in wonder.

"Some of the greatest scuba diving in the world is here in the Keys," Dirk said proudly. "Some people dive for pirate treasure in these waters. Do you dive?"

"No. I'm not that strong a swimmer. But I love snorkeling. And you can see almost as much."

"Nooo. Not quite. It's a whole other world. Diving is a lot like flying. There's a sense of freedom, of weightlessness, of all-encompassing grandeur. I can try to explain it, but it really must be experienced firsthand."

"You really love diving, don't you?" Shelley asked with a soft smile. "But I think I'll stay on top of the water. Look down there. See that big fish? That's his place. Mine is up here. I won't bother him if he doesn't bother me."

Dirk was laughing as he swung down the ladder from the flying bridge. He had stopped the engine and dropped anchor while Shelley was discussing her <u>laissez-faire</u> policy concerning fish and deep water.

She watched Dirk inflate a rubber raft, toss it over the side, jump over the side himself, and hold up his hands for the basket Nuncie had packed.

"Come on, woman. Get moving. Gather your gear and come down the ladder. Oh, and hand that paddle down to me, too, please."

After some trepidation on Shelley's part, Dirk paddled them the short distance to the island, the muscles of his broad back and shoulders moving like a smooth machine. Pulling the raft along with him when he waded ashore, he helped Shelley out, handed her the basket, and pulled the raft above the waterline. Holding the basket between them, they climbed a slight grade to sit in the shade of some fir trees.

Shelley took off the blue striped shirt she had borrowed. Looking around she said, "I expected to see the palm trees, but not these evergreens. How do they grow here so far from cool weather?"

"I don't think evergreens need cool weather. Well, not all of them, anyway. Maybe you're thinking of the kinds that get used for Christmas trees. There are evergreens on nearly all the Keys. I guess the pine cones wash ashore or the seeds blow from one island to the next. Surely you must have seen them when you drove down."

Shelley shook her head. "It was dark when I reached the Keys. All I saw was the highway, my headlight beams, and occasionally some water shining alongside the road. That was a terrible trip."

"Poor baby," Dirk said, patting her on the shoulder. Almost of its own accord, his arm crept around her shoulders and gently pulled her to him.

Shelley made no resistance. In fact, she snuggled closer. It seemed the natural thing to do.

The cruiser swung gently at anchor; the waves rippled at the shore; the birds chirped their siesta song in the trees. Shelley and Dirk were completely mesmerized. It took a giant effort for him to rouse himself enough to offer her a choice of activities, "Swim first or eat first?"

"Umm, swim first, I think."

"Okay! Let's go!" and Dirk leaped to his feet, pulling Shelley up and into the water after him with much splashing.

"Be careful where you step in the water," he called out. "Coral is sharp and you could get a bad cut, one easily infected."

Conscious of his warning, they swam and dove and played like porpoises. They finally staggered ashore, laughing and breathless, to throw themselves down in the shade. Amid much pushing and shoving, they finally had the lunch spread out on the blanket and settled back to enjoy it.

"Why does eating outside always make food taste so much better?" Shelley asked dreamily as she peeled a papaya and cut it into slices on a plate. "Those bollos were delicious. And I like tacos. Nuncie was very clever to pack all the fixings in those little dishes so we could each have ours the way we wanted to. Does she make her own salsa? I've never tasted better."

"I don't know about the salsa, but she's the world's best cook. How about bringing that papaya over here so we can share?"

When Shelley moved nearer, Dirk drew her down to lie beside him, head on his shoulder, and the plate of papaya slices resting on his stomach. Choosing a piece of fruit, he held it above her. Her mouth opened and he popped it in.

"Mm-mm. Good!"

"My turn! My turn!" Dirk teased.

Shelley picked a piece of the juicy orange fruit and moved it toward his mouth. Slippery as it was, she dropped it just at his collarbone. Quickly picking it up, she shoved it in his mouth, and leaned over to lick the juice from the base of his throat.

Dirk jackknifed up, inadvertently knocking Shelley backwards on the blanket. "Good God, woman, what are you doing?"

He could hardly breathe, the pressure in his lungs, and lower, almost cutting off his blood supply. "Have you any idea what that does to me? Where were you when they were teaching sex education?" he asked in exasperation.

Shelley lay there, blinking up at him. "I'm sorry, Dirk. I wasn't thinking. I just tried to neaten you up a little bit. You'd have been all sticky."

"Yes. Well . . . I guess I overreacted a little."

Shelley sat up and nodded. "Maybe a little."

"But I could have washed it off in the water."

"Of course," she agreed, tongue in cheek.

"In fact, maybe I'll go in the water now and cool off a little."

"Great, I'll pack the basket and gather the towels and stuff. Then I'll wander along the beach. Perhaps there'll be another pretty shell or two."

When Dirk came splashing out of the water, he found Shelley sitting primly on the blanket, sandals on, borrowed shirt on, basket packed.

"You okay?" he asked.

"Of course."

"Not angry because I reacted like a first class jerk?"

"Never," Shelley laughed.

"Well, then, . . . let's shove off."

Dirk dragged the raft to the water's edge, helped Shelley in, and paddled back to the cruiser. He held the raft steady while she went up the rope ladder that was hanging over the side of the boat.

"Looking good, Shelley! That shirt does more for you than it ever did for me." Dirk handed up the basket and climbed aboard, leaving the raft tied up to a cleat, to be deflated and repacked when they reached the marina.

He stood, staring at her where she sat in the stern. "Why is a man's shirt so darned sexy on a woman?" he asked.

"I presume that's a rhetorical question. You can't really expect me to answer that. I don't know the answer, anyhow."

"No. I guess not. But keep the shirt." Eyes smoky with desire, they narrowed as he gazed at her. His voice grew huskier as he continued, "I rather like the idea that you'll wear it now and again."

Shelley flushed prettily, but neglected to comment.

When they left the boat, Shelley appeared to be limping. Dirk, always alert to her activity, was instantly aware of her problem.

83

When they entered the Florida room, he said, "Sit here, please. Which foot is injured?"

Startled, she asked, "How did you know?"

"I warned you about the coral. Did you cut your foot while we were horsing around in the water?"

"No."

"You weren't going to tell me about it, were you?"

"No, I wasn't. I felt stupid. I didn't see the piece of coral when I was walking along looking for shells. You were right. It's sharp stuff."

"Dangerous, too. It's all too easy to get an infection from it. Take off your sandal and put your foot on the coffee table so I can disinfect it. I'll get my kit and be right back."

Returning almost instantly, he started to set out swabs, cotton balls, antiseptic ointment, an antibiotic ointment, tape . . .

Shelley drew back in horror. "It's only a little cut. You're making it look like major surgery." Dirk grunted. "What's this on your foot? A bandage?"

Shelley looked guilty. "A paper napkin. It was bleeding so hard, it was all I could find to put on it to apply pressure."

Dirk grunted again. "Grab my shoulder. This will hurt. I'll have to soak the paper off before I can clean out your cut."

Shelley stared at the ceiling, trying to think of something to distract her. "I really enjoyed today. You have a great cabin cruiser. It has an unusual name, *DOUBLE OR NOTHING*. How did you happen to give it that name?"

"A silly thing, really. One of my buddies and I had a series of long-standing bets on the Miami Dolphin games. I was so far ahead he offered me double or nothing on the Super Bowl. We had a blind draw for teams and another for point spreads. The upshot was I won. And at double the bet! . . . Move your foot over the bowl . . . It was just enough, with what I'd already saved, to buy the boat." Dirk raised his eyes from Shelley's foot and grinned. "I only named it *DOUBLE OR NOTHING* to torment Jerry." He stared off into space, frowning. "Strange. I can't get him to bet on anything lately."

Shelley laughed in spite of the stinging of her foot. It was a little better once he applied the ointment, however.

"When you go up to bed tonight, I'll carry you. You shouldn't walk on that anymore than you have too."

"No, Dirk. I'll be able to walk. Don't baby me."

"We'll see," he said.

CHAPTER FIVE

N<small>UNCIE HAD BEEN HOVERING AROUND</small>, murmuring away in Spanish, while Dirk was tending to Shelley's foot. She leaned over and, in a low voice, said a few words in his ear.

He looked up with a startled expression on his face. "Por supuesto! Gracias, Nuncie."

I'm sorry," he said to Shelley. "Nuncie reminded me that you might want to get out of your sticky bathing suit and wash the salt out of your hair." He stood up. "Let me clean up this stuff and I'll carry you upstairs."

"Really, Dirk! I can walk. I walked in from the car," she reminded him.

"No charge. Part of the service," he said, repacking his kit.

Meanwhile Nuncie had disposed of the papers and cotton balls, emptied the bowl, and rinsed it out.

"We'll wrap a plastic bag over your bandage and tape it so the water can't get inside . . . . Shower or tub? If it's tub, your foot hangs over the edge," Dirk warned.

"Shower, please. I'd like to get the salt out of my hair and I can't do that in the tub."

"Shower it is," said Dirk, bending over to lift Shelley into his arms.

She hastily struggled to her one good foot. "All right. Carry me. But no hernias or slipped disks. At least let me spare you those," she said, slipping her arms around his neck.

Clasping her in his arms, he stood looking down at her. "For a tall girl you don't weigh much."

"Give me a break, Dirk. 'Girls' are women my mother's age. I'm a woman!"

"Yes, you are, indeed," he agreed, eyes crinkling at the corners as he grinned.

Nuncie said something quietly to Dirk as he turned sidewise to go through the door on his way to the stairs.

"Bueno, Nuncie. Una idea excellente."

Up the stairs and into the bedroom Dirk carried Shelley. He slowly released her, her body sliding along his, fitting as though patterned together through time. Clasping her tightly in his arms, he buried his face in the tender joining between her shoulder and neck.

It felt wonderful; as if she had come home. But . . . Shelley was bewildered. This was too much, too soon. She had to stop him. This couldn't be happening.

"Dirk," she said, stiffening in his arms. "Dirk, please. I want to get out of this suit."

"Oh, yes, darling. Let me help you," he said thickly, reaching for the buttons on the borrowed shirt.

"Dirk! Dirk!" Shelley called again, giving his shoulder a gentle shake. "You brought me up here so I could have a shower. So I could wash my hair."

He appeared to be awakening from a dream, eyes smoky, breathing irregular. "Yes. Yes, of course. Your shower."

Nuncie entered the room with some plastic and tape as Dirk was backing away from Shelley, still appearing dazed.

Shelley sank to the edge of the bed, while Dirk dropped to his knees to wrap her injured foot. He finished the wrapping, and, recovering himself, he offered his robe, ". . . to wear after your shower. I'll wait until you come out, and I'll remove the plastic.

It will be too awkward for you to do. Nuncie suggested you get into bed and she'll bring some supper up on a tray."

Shelley shook her head. "I don't want to cause all that trouble. I'm sure I can manage the plastic and my nightie is right here. I'll be fine."

Pulling her nightgown from under the pillow, she hobbled into the bathroom and closed the door firmly.

Dirk ran his fingers through his hair, head bowed in chagrin. What ailed him? Why was he acting like an inexperienced teenager with his first adolescent crush? Damn! He had been more poised with his first love! Love? How could it be love? They had only known each other for three days! He was the one who needed the shower, and a good cold one at that.

Passing the bathroom door, hearing the water running and Shelley splashing, Dirk decided his cold shower was not at all remiss, especially when her splashing raised visions that put his blood pressure on overload.

Shelley was ensconced against pillows stacked at the head of the bed and sipping a cup of hot coffee when Dirk returned to her room. He was wearing the robe she had spurned, the navy blue toweling darkening his eyes to a deep charcoal gray.

Nuncie bustled in with Shelley's dinner on a tray, which she proceeded to put across her lap. Shaking Shelley's napkin out and spreading it on her chest, she gave a directive to Dirk and both of them left the room.

Within minutes they returned, Nuncie carrying a TV table which she set up near the bed. Dirk followed her with another dinner on a tray. Putting it on the little table, he moved the aqua chair over, sat, shook out his napkin, and picked up his fork.

"All the comforts of home," he said, white teeth flashing against his tanned skin. After taking one bite of the succulent crab cake, he stood up and strolled toward the bed. Shelley stared at him, eyes wide in apprehension.

"I thought we'd have some dinner music," he said, snapping on the bedside radio. He stood looking down at her, a half-smile playing around his lips. "Did you think I was going to jump your bones?" he asked seriously.

Shelley swallowed the food that had been lodged in her mouth and shook her head.

"Good. I usually give a warning before I do that."

Shelley glanced up quickly and was relieved to see the glimmer of a smile deep in his eyes, the softness of his mouth assuring her she was safe for the time being. He went back to his chair to finish eating, intermittently fussing over Shelley as much as Nuncie did.

She pushed away half her dessert, a blissful praline cheese cake that had her in transports.

"If you're so mad about the cheese cake, why don't you finish it?" Dirk asked.

"No room. No room," Shelley lamented, patting her tummy. "I'm willing but it won't fit."

Dirk was laughing when he put both trays and the small folding table out in the hall. Returning, he said, "There's a special on TV this evening, an historical perspective of life in the Middle Ages. Would you care to watch it?"

"Yes, I would, but I don't want you to carry me downstairs. I can walk."

"No need. There's a set in my room. Let me help you," he said, walking toward the bed.

Shelley drew back, eyes wary.

Dirk's insides reacted strongly, yelling wildly, "Crimus, woman! You'd think I had rape on my mind!"

But the cool lawyer took over, asking softly, "Shelley? Is there something else you'd rather watch?"

Shelley knew he was angry. In spite of his restrained question, she could see his eyes were a cold gray, as dark as shards of deep-water ice.

She shook her head. "No. That's fine."

"Good," he continued almost as softly. "There's a big overstuffed armchair where you can sit. We'll put your foot up on the ottoman so it won't throb, and we'll watch the program."

Shelley finished the last of her coffee. Sneaking a look at his eyes, which seemed to have defrosted somewhat, she said, "Thank you. I'd like that."

About halfway through the program, Nuncie appeared with a bowl of popcorn for each of them, making some comment about it being like the 'cinema'. She tossed, "Buenos noches, niños" over her shoulder as she left to retire for the night.

When the program was over, Dirk helped Shelley back into her bedroom. She had been using Dirk's shirt as a robe over her nightie and she stood, waiting for him to leave, before she took it off. Realizing what was delaying her, he turned his back.

It was an uncomfortable situation. When Shelley gathered he wasn't leaving, she quickly put his shirt on the end of the bed and got beneath the covers, sheet pulled up so only the straps of her nightie showed.

Dirk walked over to say goodnight but stood watching her instead.

Shelley decided it was up to her. "Good night, Dirk. Thank you for tending to my foot. It feels better already."

Nodding as he sat down on the bed, he reached for the hand that was outside the covers. He <u>had</u> to touch her. He'd been good for over four hours. Certainly helping her across the hallway didn't count.

He picked up her hand, threading his fingers through hers, feeling perfectly content. Leaning forward, he rested his right hand along the other side of her hips. Slowly, trancelike, he swayed toward her, eyes on her lips.

Shelley could no more prevent the kiss than she could hold back the tide, nor did she want to. All the tension that had been simmering for two days diminished as their lips touched. It was so right. It was so natural. It was where she wanted to be.

For Dirk the kiss was soon not enough. He needed to taste her, to hold her to him, to feel her silken skin beneath his hands. He slipped his tongue between her lips, sipping, testing, encouraged by the soft little sounds in Shelley's throat.

He slid his arms around her, raising her from the pillows, cuddling her against his chest. One of Shelley's hands went around his neck, the other nestled against his chest.

Dirk's satisfied moan brought her to her senses. Ignoring the way the tendrils of dark hair curled around her fingers, she pushed at his chest, tearing her mouth from under his.

"Dirk. Stop. We're practically strangers. What about Marilee, the woman you're dating? What about Rob?"

Dirk watched her lips, still glistening from his kisses. "I don't feel like a stranger. We don't feel like strangers. I feel as if I've known you forever."

"Yes. I understand what you're saying, but I'm here under a police order. I'm not a guest. I'm not a friend. Please understand how difficult this is for me. We just cannot get involved."

Dirk ran both hands through his dark wavy hair. "You're right. I'm taking advantage of you. However," he continued with his lawyer's logic, "I'm not sorry. I'll respect your wishes until this mess is cleared up. But be warned, Shelley, it's not over between us. It may never be."

Shelley's eyes widened as he strode from the room, closing the door firmly behind him. One couldn't mistake his warning. The sooner she could hit the road, the safer she'd feel . . . . And the safer she'd be!

Bright and early the next morning, Shelley was at the breakfast table. Not exactly 'bright', she was thinking. Having spent a very restless night, she could be forgiven for hoping Dirk had, too.

With a smaller bandage on her cut, Shelley was able to wear her sandals. There was no other choice but her coral suit and silk blouse. Her lack of a restful sleep and change of clothing affected her attitude; her normal optimism had deserted her; she saw only gloom ahead. She would probably end up going to jail . . . probably for twenty years . . . and all because she tried to help her mother.

Dirk came into the room just as Shelley's tears threatened to overflow. Turning quickly to watch a bird fly through the yard, she surreptitiously wiped her eyes.

A pang of guilt smote Dirk. His restless night had been filled with disgust at himself. My God! He was thirty-one years old. Where was his control? How could he have acted in such an ungentlemanly fashion to a woman entrusted to his care? Should he apologize? Did what he said last night count? But that was no apology! Did he really say he wasn't sorry?

Dirk Gentile, the iceberg lawyer in the courtroom, was hot and bothered about a lawbreaker, a trespasser, a would-be thief! Praise God, his father would never hear about this. But Hollis, good old Hollis . . . he'd never let any qualms hold him back. Dirk cringed mentally. Hollis had probably already been in touch with his dad. Small towns were bad enough . . . all right, small city, 25,000 is good sized, . . . but when that city is on an island . . . .

"How is your foot, Shelley? Did it keep you awake?"

"It's fine. No problem. I put a small bandage on it this morning. It's okay, honest."

"You don't look as if you slept very well. I'm sorry if I'm responsible. I never meant to upset you."

Shelley nodded her head a couple of times, studiously avoiding Dirk's eyes. "Yes. Well . . . . I guess I'm worried about today," she said mendaciously. She'd die before she'd let Dirk Gentile think _he_ had upset _her_! Why did she have to keep reminding herself he was the enemy, the handsomest pirate she'd ever seen? All he lacked was the gold hoop in his ear. He didn't even need the red head scarf. Ah, well, this would soon be over and she'd be safely on her way home. Belatedly she added, 'and with the necklace.'

Dirk took a few sips of coffee. Putting his cup down, he reached across and took Shelley's cold hand in his warm one. "Don't be worried about today," he said. "It's a formality, really. Your clearance from Orlando must have come through by now, holiday or not. Our appointment's at ten."

Shelley's hand jerked. Then she turned it over and gripped Dirk's hand. "What will the judge do?" she asked.

"It's a formality," he repeated. "We'll go into his chambers, his office in the courthouse, and he'll ask us both some questions. Hollis will be there, too, I imagine. Just answer his questions truthfully. Everything should be all right."

"What will he ask me?" Shelley's cheeks paled at the thought.

"Every judge has his own method. I think Judge Haley's covering this week. He's a great person. He went to school with my mother, Miami U. She did social services; he did law."

Shelley looked out through the screening, catching a flicker of red feathers in the evergreens. Sighing to herself, she wondered if anyone on this island was on her side.

"Do you think you can walk?" Dirk asked. "It's only a few blocks and it's a beautiful morning."

"Unless you'd rather ride a bike?" he added as an afterthought. "You could borrow Nuncie's. We won't be gone that long."

Seeing her hesitation, he shrugged. "We could drive, but we might end up walking just as far. The tourists use up all the parking spaces."

She smiled slightly. "Fine. We'll walk. I'm sure I can handle it."

Shelley was tall, but Dirk was taller. And he was a walker! After two blocks, she stopped to regain her breath, shake her foot, and remove her jacket. While removing it, a button caught in her long blond hair.

Dirk stopped and returned to help her untangle it. Shelley noticed his hands were trembling. Raising her eyes, she met the soft melting look that had almost been her undoing the night before. Her breath caught in her throat. Dirk froze, fingers twisted in her hair, eyes locked with hers. They stood, lost in each other, until a truck passing in the street brought them back to their surroundings.

Hair untangled, Shelley found her hand in Dirk's as they continued on.

Before long they came to the historic old orange brick Victorian Court House on the corner of Angela and Whitehead. When

Shelley started to turn into the main entrance, Dirk stopped her. He indicated a newer building beyond it. "They moved into this building about ten years ago. Some people call it the New Court House. Others say Court House Annex. But everybody'd know which one you mean."

He steered her toward the steps. "The jail was moved here, too. It's up on the second floor. That's where the guards have their quarters."

He could have left out that part about the jail as far as Shelley was concerned. She had felt Dirk turn her down a left hand corridor and lead her to a bench. She had not even been aware of entering the building!

She felt the impression of marble floors, heavy wooden doors with brightly polished brass handles, and a mixture of paneling and beige walls where portraits of somber-looking men in black judicial robes stared solemnly down.

Seated on the bench, she watched Hollis and Dirk carry on a whispered conversation. Hollis seemed to be quite definite about what he was saying, nodding his head, and then shaking it while he grabbed Dirk's arm and talked earnestly into his face. Dirk had his back to her. She knew that meant trouble, and probably for her.

A white haired man in a short sleeved shirt opened the heavy door across from Shelley. He gave a courtly bow of his head and his eyes crinkled at the corners as he said, "Good morning, ma'am."

Dirk and Hollis turned and made for the door, Dirk stopping to grasp Shelley firmly by the elbow to lead her into the room.

Judge Haley paused in the act of donning his judicial robe to acknowledge Shelley's introduction to him. Straightening his robe, he moved behind his desk, indicating they should be seated in the three chairs in front of it. Seeing Shelley eye his large desk, which definitely showed the nicks and scrapes of long and hard wear, he smiled. "This was my great-granddaddy's desk. He was a state senator along about the time the old Court House was built. It's seen a lot of history on this Key," he said as he patted the desk fondly.

Shelley nodded in assent.

He indicated the floor-to-ceiling bookcases around the room. "A lot of those books were his." He smiled at her amazement. "Not all. There are some new ones, too. We keep up with what's going on, even out here at the end of the U.S." He chuckled.

At Shelley's smile, he pointed at the wall behind her. "That's him. Enos Q. Haley, III." When she turned to look at the portrait of the dignified gentleman, the judge muttered, "A scallywag, that one." In a louder voice, he said, "Our family's been here a long time. About as long as Hollis' and Dirk's."

As Dirk and Hollis exchanged glances, the kindly Enos Haley straightened in his chair and became Judge Enos Quintus Haley VI, presiding in chambers. He reached for the glasses on his desk and adjusted the wire stems over his ears. Pulling several papers toward him, he leafed through them, looking over his glasses at Shelley or at Dirk. Even Hollis came in for a long stare.

Turning to Shelley, he asked, "You're from Orlando, Miss Morgan?"

"Yes, sir," she answered nervously.

"We haven't been able to check with your place of business, because of the weekend and the holiday, and no one answers at your home."

"No, sir. I live alone. The magazine should be open now, though." She turned distractedly to Dirk, who had hissed, "Your honor," at her. When she continued staring, he whispered, "Not 'sir'; 'your honor'."

Shelley flushed in embarrassment.

The judge had watched the by-play, and waved his hand in dismissal. "They're checking on it. We should hear shortly." After a pause, he flapped a sheet of paper and continued, "This is a serious charge, Miss Morgan. You are, what . . . 25, 26?"

"Twenty-six, your honor."

"Yes. Far past the age of teenage hi-jinx." Shelley's eyes flicked to Dirk. He had a frown on his face. Oh, lordy, this was getting worse by the minute.

"Chief Mitchum explained why you're not being charged with 'Breaking and Entering'. It seems a door was unlocked?" He nodded questioningly at Shelley.

Shelley's head bobbed in return.

"May I ask why you entered Mr. Gentile's premises?"

Shelley glanced at Dirk, who was staring stoically ahead. Feeling abandoned, though why she should Shelley didn't know, she lowered her head and almost whispered, "He has something belonging to my mother. She'd like it back."

The judge's eyebrows arched in surprise. "Mr. Gentile has property belonging to your mother which he refuses to return?"

Under the judge's incredulous stare, Dirk moved uneasily in his seat. "It's not quite that simple, your honor."

"Ah, yes," Judge Haley said, leaning back heavily in his creaking chair. "It rarely is." He sighed deeply, then peered searchingly at Shelley. "Will you and Chief Mitchum step into the corridor for a few minutes, please, while I talk with Mr. Gentile?"

Shelley and Hollis walked to the door. When she turned to look at Dirk, he was staring at the floor. Feeling very subdued, she went back to her former place on the bench.

Hollis stood silently beside her. Where was the jovial policeman of Saturday night? Had Dirk been right? Was everybody taking this more seriously than she thought they should? Or maybe she wasn't taking this seriously enough. Shelley rubbed her forehead, but it did not relieve the pressure of her headache.

Five minutes stretched to ten, that ten to fifteen, before Judge Haley opened the door to invite them back into his chambers.

When everyone was again seated, Judge Haley leaned forward on his desk, arms folded, and looked searchingly at Shelley, at Dirk, and finally at Hollis.

Hollis was the only one to meet the judge's eyes.

Giving one more cool survey of the three in front of the desk, the judge sat back in his chair. "There seems to be something I am missing here. Edward, will you and Hollis have a seat in the corridor. I'd like to talk to Miss Morgan further."

Shelley shot a frightened, questioning glance, at Dirk. He put his hand on her shoulder and squeezed gently. "It'll be all right," he said in a low voice. "Just tell him the truth."

After the door clicked shut behind them, Judge Haley leaned forward again, index finger of one hand curved over his mouth, thumb under his chin, gazing out the window beside his desk. Turning back to Shelley, he said, "Tell me in your own words what has happened to bring us to this hearing."

"You've seen Chief Mitchum's report?"

The judge nodded. "I want to hear your story."

"Well . . . ." After a slow beginning, the words tumbled from Shelley. "My mother was bored, my stepfather travels on business, she lost money playing bridge, she didn't want to tell Frank, that's my stepfather, that she gave a necklace belonging to him as security for the debt, she decided she wanted the necklace returned so she could put it back, so I came to get it." Shelley, breathless, sat back in her chair, not realizing she had gravitated toward the judge in her earnestness.

"You came to get it," the judge repeated. "Just like that?"

"Well, no." She paused. "I went to see Hugh Donovan, the club owner in Orlando, to ask him for the necklace and give him a promissory note or tell him that my mother would borrow the money from a bank or something, but Mr. Gentile had already collected it for safe keeping."

Shelley stopped to think. She did not want to put Dirk in an unfavorable light. Biting her lips in thought, she began again. "Mr. Gentile had flown up to pick up the necklace. Mr. Donovan gave me his card. I drove to his office in Miami."

"From Orlando?"

"Yes, sir."

"When was this?'

"Friday, your honor."

The judge nodded. "Please continue."

"When I got to his office, he wasn't there. He'd flown directly here to Key West. So I drove to Key West. It was too late Friday night to contact him so I checked into a motel and called him in the morning. Mr. Gentile saw me at two o'clock Saturday but he couldn't reach Mr. Donovan to get permission to give me the necklace."

"Why would he consider giving you the necklace?" Judge Haley asked.

"Mr. Donovan said anything Dirk decided was all right with him."

"Did you get that in writing?"

"No, your honor."

"Ah," he breathed. "Go on."

"We'll, that's about it."

"The trespassing," he reminded gently.

"Oh, yes. The trespassing." Shelley bit her lip again. She did not want to say anything about Dirk receiving stolen property, though why she wanted to shield him she didn't know. He was holding her against her will and causing all this problem . . . . Well maybe she was a little to blame.

"I went back to the motel. I got to thinking. I decided everybody would be happier if I got the necklace back. Mom could return it. Frank wouldn't find out about it—I'd leave a note in its place, promising to make restitution. I figured that wouldn't really be stealing."

The judge raised his eyes from where he had been doodling on the desk. He looked at her in fascination, amazed at the machinations of her mind, the convoluted logic. Why did he feel, though, that something was being left out?"

"Who is your stepfather?"

"His name's Francis D. Wilson, a retired Air Force colonel. He does consulting for the aircraft industry."

"And what is it you don't want him to find out?"

Shelley squirmed in her chair. Either her mother or she was going to go to jail. She continued haltingly, "Frank has several very old necklaces in a safe deposit box. Mom borrowed one."

"Borrowed one? She has access to the box."

"Yes, your honor."

"A key?"

"Yes, sir"

"The box is in her name, too?"

"I think so, sir."

The judge nodded as if one piece of the puzzle had fallen into place. With an abrupt change of subject, he asked, "Is your stepfather from up St. Augustine way?"

"I think so, your honor. At least he has a brother there. He came to their wedding."

"Yes. Walter Raleigh Wilson. Owns TV stations in Northern Florida. Went to law school with him," the judge mused.

Shelley raised her eyes heavenward. Good grief! Does everybody in Key West know everybody in Florida!

The judge continued, "There've been rumors flying around for years of how their family received the necklaces. Do you know the true story?"

"I know what Frank told us when he showed them to us. One of his ancestors sailed with Drake. The necklaces were among the jewels liberated from some Spanish ships in the sixteenth century. The ship his ancestor was on went back to England while Drake and his ship, the Golden Hind, went up the west coast of South America. His family received the necklaces as a reward for service to Queen Elizabeth, for helping to secure so much wealth for England."

"That's what the rumors were." Judge Haley smiled as he nodded. "It seems there was a title, and estates, too, but the title was dropped and the estates disposed of before his family came to Florida. About 200 years ago, maybe less."

He was silent for a moment. "You've seen them?"

"Yes, sir. They have heavy antique settings, but they're finely detailed. Three are gold. The fourth is silver, but tarnished. They have large, mostly rough-cut stones: rubies, emeralds from Colombia, diamonds from northern South America, a few sapphires. They're encrusted with pearls and diamonds."

"Yes. That's what I'd heard, that they were unbelievable. No wonder your mother wants to replace that necklace in the safe deposit box. I imagine a museum would love to obtain one of them. Even one of the jewels."

"Yes, sir. But Frank feels they're family jewels. They should stay in the family."

"A very romantic tale." The judge had a far-away dream in his eyes. "We tend to forget those adventures of the high seas. They were bread and meat to us when we were boys."

He rose and stood looking out the window for a moment. Giving a heavy sigh, he walked to the door and opened it. "Come in, gentlemen," he said.

CHAPTER SIX

DIRK GAVE SHELLEY A QUESTIONING look before seating himself and picking up her hand. Hollis sat on the other side of Shelley, running his finger around his uniform collar and pulling his jacket straight.

After surveying each of the participants, the judge swiveled in his chair to again face the window. Finally he turned to the shelf behind his desk and removed a heavy cream-colored tome. Opening it, he peered over his glasses at them again. "I will quote from this law book." Leafing through until he found the page, he began, "'Most infractions of law are not judged as crimes unless they were accompanied by a "criminal state of mind". This question of mental inclination is not so important in the case of routine petty offenses'," he continued, staring at Dirk over his glasses. "'But when the charge is a misdemeanor (or a felony), the accused must generally be proved to have had a criminal state of mind to be found guilty'."

He closed the book firmly and set it aside. "I believe you did not have a 'criminal state of mind', Miss Morgan, when you entered Dirk Edward's home. Trespassing, however, is a misdemeanor. As long as Mr. Gentile persists in pressing charges, I have no recourse but to warn you not to leave this jurisdiction, at least until we hear from Tallahassee and Orlando."

Shelley jerked her hand from Dirk's and turned toward him with a gasp. "Pressing charges! You told me this would be a mere formality!"

Shelley clutched her stomach as nausea hit her. She swallowed nervously. No, it wasn't nausea. It was a feeling of betrayal! How could this be happening?

"You told me not to worry," she cried. "I trusted you!"

Dirk flushed, but said nothing, staring straight ahead.

Judge Haley waited with a frown on his face, then continued, "I gathered there was a doubt concerning the legality of Mrs. Wilson's using the necklace, belonging to her husband, as security for her debt. It would seem, on the surface, no larceny has been committed intentionally, again the 'criminal intent' clause. The safe deposit box appears to be in both names and Mrs. Wilson has a key, which allowed access to the box with her husband's implied permission."

The judge looked from Shelley to Dirk, and back again. "However, the necklace was given into Mr. Donovan's hands as security, a verbal contract as it were. The next decision must be his."

Judge Haley stood in dismissal. When the others also stood, he said, "When my office receives confirmation of the information we need, we will be in touch with you."

The three turned to walk out the door, Hollis guiding Shelley, who appeared to be in a daze.

"Shelley," Dirk pleaded.

"No!" she shouted hoarsely, holding up her hands to ward him off. "No! Don't touch me! Don't talk to me!"

Hollis shook his head at Dirk. "Come, Miss Shelley. Let me buy you a cup of coffee. It'll give you time to gather yourself."

Dirk frowned as he watched them walk toward the elevator.

When they were seated in the coffee shop in the basement of the courthouse, hot coffee in front of them, Shelley was still numb.

"I don't know what ails Dirk Edward," Hollis began. "A nice young lady like you. I admit we were trying to give you a warning on Saturday night. But to press a trespassin' charge . . . It appeared he cared about you." Hollis stared into his coffee. "I don't understand that boy. Don't rightly know how his daddy'll take this, either."

"Yes, well, I don't know how my mother's going to be taking this! Every time I've talked to her, and it's been nearly every day, I just told her I was taking a few days off. That, 'No, I didn't have the necklace yet, but anytime now'. I'm going to have to tell her the whole story." Shelley shook her head and firmed her lips. "I can't. I just can't."

Hollis patted her shoulder. "Would you like a sweet roll or a piece of dessert?" he asked her by way of comfort.

With tears in her eyes, Shelley gave him a brilliant smile. "No, thank you, Chief Mitchum. Not right now."

"Call me Hollis," he said, patting her hand. Turning away, he mumbled, "Gotta be insane, that boy."

"I should've had a lawyer," Shelley said loudly.

"Prob'ly should," Hollis agreed. Then he thought for a minute. "Though no reason to think so in advance, Missy. Not the way Dirk Edward was actin' like your lawyer the other night."

Shelley took a sip of coffee, feeling its warmth slip inside. "That's true . . . but I just can't fathom this. How could he press charges? He knows I didn't mean any harm."

"That makes two of us, Miss Shelley. And I'm not so sure Dirk Edward understands it, either."

"What I really don't understand," Shelley said, "is the identification part. No one's at home at my apartment in

Orlando, granted. But Tallahassee, . . . you should be able to get through to the magazine in Tallahassee."

"No, ma'am." Hollis shook his head. "Big tropical storm came in off the Gulf. Electricity out for sure. Even phone lines out. Tried the Fax machine, too, but no phones, no electricity equals no Fax. Guess the businesses are pretty well closed down."

"Temporarily, that is," he added as an afterthought.

Shelley pushed her half-full cup away from her. "I have to call my mother. God knows I don't want to, but I may as well get it over with."

Standing up, Hollis said, "Come along, Missy. I'll drive you back to Dirk's. Nuncie'll fuss over you. Make you feel better."

"No," Shelley said firmly. "I can not go back there. I'll go back to the motel."

"Motels are costly," Hollis warned. "I have a friend, runs a Bed and Breakfast. Long as you have to stay here, might as well be among friends. Down in town, too, where things are goin' on."

"Oh, Hollis, thank you. I really could use a friend."

"That's okay, Missy. Feel kinda responsible. Though I was only doin my job, mind."

"I know. No hard feelings. I don't know whose fault it is. I've got a list of about five names, but that doesn't help."

"Guess not. Well, come along, Miss Shelley. We'll get your stuff from Dirk Edward's and I'll take you over to Lilabelle's."

Two minutes in the chief's patrol car and they were in front of Gentile's.

"My car's in the yard, Hollis. Tell me where your friend's house is and I'll drive myself over."

"Nope. I'll wait. You can follow me. You need a full scale introduction to your new friend."

Shelley turned away with tears in her eyes, got out of the car, and walked through the gate. Nuncie answered the doorbell and ushered Shelley inside, clucking and fuming, yet obviously pleased that Shelley would be remaining in town.

Shelley walked toward the stairs and started up. "I'm just here to pick up my things, Nuncie. I have to stay in town, but I'm not going to stay here."

The study door opened violently and Dirk stood silently in the doorway, watching Shelley.

She paused, staring over her shoulder at him. Turning her back, she continued up the steps.

"Shelley, please."

"No."

"Shelley. Let me talk to you. Let me explain."

"You can't say anything I want to hear."

By now Dirk was about four steps behind Shelley as she continued upward. He grasped her hand, stopping her and turning her toward him.

"Shelley, I never wanted to hurt you. Come into the study so we can talk."

Her eyes flicked over his shoulder to where Nuncie was standing at the foot of the staircase, gripping the newell post, and listening avidly.

"Shelley, talk to me. I love you."

"Hah!"

"Come into the library. Please. Listen to me. Then if you want to leave, I won't stop you.

Shelley stood looking down at him, his face lifted toward her, both hands lifted, as if in supplication. It would have taken a harder heart than hers to refuse. She sighed, pulled her hand free, and nodded.

Dirk turned, unable to speak, and led the way into the library.

Shelley stood just inside the door, refusing to be seated, hands gripped tightly at her waist.

Dirk paced.

He stopped in front of her, but she refused to meet his eyes. Pushing his fingers through his dark hair, his handsome features tautened by strain, he turned away to begin pacing again.

He stopped across the room from her, loosening his tie and unbuttoning the top two buttons on his shirt. Swallowing heavily, he tried to speak.

"Well?" Shelley prompted. "Hollis is waiting. He's going to take me to his friend's Bed and Breakfast."

"I don't want you to leave," Dirk said abruptly, raising his firm chin. "I want you to stay here."

"Tough! I have to stay in Key West. I do <u>not</u> have to stay in this house."

"Honey, listen to me. The only reason I pressed charges was to have you stay a few more days. I didn't want you to leave. I wanted us to have a chance to know each other better."

This was a new thought for Shelley. There was no malice intended? He wanted her to stay? But the feeling of betrayal had gone too deep to be easily soothed.

With a toss of her head, she said, "You're messing with my life, Dirk. My mother is a nervous wreck. I've got deadlines to meet. And you're playing games!"

He turned away to walk again. "They call me 'The Iceberg', or 'The Iceman' in the courtroom. Nothing ruffles me." He paced around the desk, pausing in front of her. "I can't explain what ails me. I know I'm acting irrationally. Believe me, I've never acted like this before."

Shelley met his eyes, before turning hastily away.

"Shelley," he said softly. "My love." He swallowed a lump in his throat. "No one has ever affected me as you do." His voice broke.

Shelley raised a hand toward him, then dropped it to her side.

"I love you," he said, tears in his eyes.

She turned her face away, hesitating before saying quietly, "You have a strange way of showing it."

He reached for her hands, pulling her gently toward him. Raising her fingers to his lips, he kissed them. Cradling them against his cheek, he pleaded, "Give me another chance. Don't leave me. Stay here until the clearance for your ID comes through."

"I don't think so." She pulled her hands free.

"Nuncie will chaperone us. I'll behave."

"I don't know," she said haltingly.

Sensing that she was wavering, Dirk promised, "I'll be your friend. I'll try to keep my hands off you. We'll spend the time doing touristy things. Let me show you my island."

"I need my head examined," Shelley mumbled to herself. Aloud, she said, "Hollis has already called his friend."

"That's easy to rectify," he said, taking heart. "I'll talk to him. Do you mind?" Grabbing her hands, he kissed them again. Raising his head, he looked at her lips.

"No," she said quietly.

He nodded, dropped her hands, and headed for the front door . . . and Hollis.

Shelley stood silently staring after Dirk, realizing she had tacitly agreed to stay with him. She shook her head. Dirk wasn't the only one acting irrationally.

Leaving Dirk and Hollis to their discussion, Shelley again started up the stairs. She wondered at every step what she could tell her mother that would set her mind at ease. She was especially concerned about how much she could tell her without the whole truth coming out.

She was sitting on the bed, hand on the phone, trying to gain courage, when there was a tap at the door.

Dirk was standing there when she opened the door. She did not step back, nor did she ask him in.

"Yes?" she said, when he made no attempt to speak.

Dirk's high cheekbones flushed, knowing her coolness was well deserved. "Hollis understands that I need to make amends. He also understands I can explain better if you stay here. He'll tell Lilabelle."

Hollis understood all that? Shelley could not conceive of the Hollis she had been talking with changing sides so quickly. But on the other hand, who was she to be questioning Hollis? Wasn't she standing here!

She nodded at Dirk and started to close the door. "Wait!" he said, putting his hand up to stop it. His eloquent eyes roamed over Shelley's face. "I want to tell you how happy it makes me to see you here."

Shelley nodded again and stepped back.

Dirk said softly, almost in a whisper, "I didn't realize it before, but when I dreamed of a woman here, my woman, she had your beautiful face, your touchable blonde hair, your tawny eyes." He opened his mouth to continue, but closed it, and walked away.

Shelley closed the door, then turned and rested against it. What kind of spell was he weaving around her? She leaned her head back and closed her eyes. It had to be some sort of Caribbean voodoo. How could she allow him to bewitch her when she knew he was continuing to press charges? Shaking her head in bewilderment, Shelley returned to the bed, and the phone.

She sat and pondered. Her mother might act like a ditz, but underneath all the fuss and dramatics, she was a pretty savvy lady. One false word and her mom would be on red alert.

Shelley dialed the number, still worrying, half hoping her mother would not be home. But she was.

"Hi, Mom. It's me."

"Michelle, love! Are you home? Do you have the necklace? Are you tired? Did you have much trouble?"

"Mom! Mom!' Shelley tried to break into the flow of words. "Mom, I'm still in Key West."

"Key West? Do you have the necklace?"

"No, Mom. Dirk feels he can't release the necklace without Hugh Donovan's say so and he can't get hold of him. Hugh's on vacation."

"Oh, Michele. What a bother this has been for you. Well, it can't be helped now. Come home, dear. I'll just have to face Frank with the whole story."

"I'm sorry, Mother." After a pause she said, "Um, Mom . . . there's a slight problem. Nothing for you to worry about," she added hastily. "Ah, you see, I can't come home right away. It might be a couple of days."

"Can't come home, Michelle? Are you having trouble with your car?"

"Not exactly."

"Honey, what's the matter?"

"Now, don't worry. I can't exactly leave Key West right now. You see, when I tried to get the necklace back on Saturday night, I was caught trespassing."

"Trespassing? Where were you trespassing?"

"At Mr. Gentile's, the lawyer."

"You were trespassing on that man's property?"

"Sort of, mom."

"What do you mean, 'sort of'?'"

"There was this door that was unlocked."

"Yes?"

"Well, I went in. But the house had a silent alarm system. They found me before I could find the necklace."

There was a deep silence on Kate's end of the phone. Shelley took that opportunity to say, "Mr. Gentile signed the complaint." There was an uneasy pause. "He's pressing charges."

"Charges! You broke into that man's house!"

"In a manner of speaking, Mom. Anyhow, they're trying to get through to Tallahassee to get a character reference from my boss. It seems a tropical storm hit up there and they can't get through."

"Yes," said her mother distractedly, "we got the edge of it, heavy rain, some wind damage . . . . Michelle, are you in jail?"

"No, Mother, I'm not, honestly. I'm staying with Mr. Gentile and his housekeeper. It's only a formality, really; however, I can't leave until my ID is checked out."

"From what I gather from the news on TV, all the businesses are closed. The repair crews are making good headway in spite of the rain, but don't expect to hear anything before tomorrow, and probably not before Thursday", her mother said in a distant voice.

There was a quiet moment. "Let me give you this phone number," Shelley said. "Call me if you need to."

"Thank you. What are you doing for clothes, dear? You certainly weren't prepared for a stay of this length when you left home."

"I picked up some things at the drug store and at a boutique in town. I'll make do. Even bought a bikini," Shelley said with a short laugh.

"May as well enjoy your captivity, eh?" Kate said, little realizing how close her choice of words came. She joined Shelley's laughter, then sobered. "I'm so sorry, dear. I've been a real problem, haven't I?"

"Oh, no, Mom. I love you. It will all work out."

"Let's hope so, Michelle. Let's hope so."

"Is Frank home this week?" Shelley asked.

"No. He's out in Seattle. He'll be home tomorrow night. He has to fly out for a consultation in Texas on Friday, but he should be back that evening."

"That'll be nice, having him home tomorrow." Shelley cleared her throat. "I must go, Mom. I'll be talking to you. Bye-bye."

"Good-bye, Michelle. I know you'll be home soon."

Shelley sat, hand on the receiver, reviewing the conversation. That had not been too bad. Her mother seemed to have taken it very well, considering she had been told much more than she had known before. Shelley drew a deep breath. Yes, her mother had taken everything quite calmly.

She went over to the closet. Time to get out of the coral suit and into her sundress. She was straightening the straps when there was a knock on the door.

Hoping it was Nuncie, she found Dirk instead.

"Nuncie sent me up to tell you lunch is ready."

"Thank you, Dirk, but I'm not hungry."

"Nuncie will have a fit. Everything's ready. Come down and try to eat, to please her." He stared beyond her into the room. "You can't stay up here the whole time. That isn't good, either."

"You're right," she agreed. "I'll come down."

Shelley found eating not too much of a strain. Dirk exerted himself to be a charming and amusing companion. He entertained her with stories of law school and his first days of practice. But it was when he began talking about the early history of Key West that Shelley began listening in earnest.

"Early in its history, because it was so far south and because ships going to South America sailed by it, Key West was a base of operations against pirates. There weren't any concrete pier or buttresses in those days, just wild rocky shores and sandy beaches."

Seeing Shelley's wide-eyed interest, he said slyly, "I hope I'm not boring you. I don't always know when to stop if I'm talking about Key West."

"No, no. I find it very interesting. Don't stop."

"After the pirates were disposed of and privateering was no longer profitable, and frowned on besides, the residents turned to salvage operations. The locals called it 'the wrecking business'."

"I've heard of the wreckers on the Cornish coast and the southern coast of England. They set fires to lure ships onto the rocks. Is that how it was done here?"

"Oh my, no," Dirk said, with a twinkle in his eye. "It was a legal occupation. They salvaged the ships that ran aground in storms, and on moonless nights, and such." He raised his hand as Shelley started to interrupt. "Wrecking licenses were issued. In fact, there were Rules of Wrecking that had to be adhered to. We can go into the Oldest House, which is a museum now, and you'll be able to see the rules for yourself. At one time, around the middle of the nineteenth century, Key West had the highest per capita income of any city in the United States, mostly from this perfectly legal industry."

"Are you pulling my leg, Dirk?'

"No, but that's an interesting thought."

Shelley immediately froze.

Dirk hurried on, "We have some time today. Can you ride a bike? Do you feel like going to visit a couple of places now?"

"Yes, I can ride a bike, and yes, I'd like to see more of the Key, too." Shelley was thinking she might as well spend her time out among people. Dirk's power would be diluted. It would be much safer.

"Great! We can go down Duval to the Oldest House and back up Whitehead to the Audubon House. We'll borrow Nuncie's bike. She won't be using it this time of day. Mine's out back, too. Then we'll be off. That's all we can fit in to visit today. Nuncie'll have dinner ready when we get back."

Standing on the 'landlubber's tilt' in the old Captain's office, listening as the guide described the ship's hatch in the roof of the Oldest House, Shelley found herself enjoying the chance to inspect Dirk's sparkling eyes, crinkled with interest, as he listened to the speaker. She was fascinated by the way his red knit shirt molded his broad shoulders. Her fingers twitched to stroke the skin of his powerful arms. She found herself growing short of breath at the movements in his shoulder and upper arm as he raised one hand to adjust his collar.

Feeling the touch of her glance upon him, Dirk turned, and everything stopped. No movement. No sound. No breathing. Only the two of them, connected across the room by the caress of a gaze that froze them in time.

The shuffling of the other tourists leaving the room roused them from the spell that had captured them. Without breaking eye contact, Dirk moved to her side, taking her arm, and following the crowd out into the garden.

Her breathing did not return to normal until they were in the kitchen, a separate cookhouse in the garden. When the others left, Dirk moved over in front of her, standing close enough that she could see the individual inky lashes that surrounded his clear silver eyes, eyes that seemed never to tire of looking at her. Again her breath stopped as she stared up at him. Realizing she had his complete attention, she dropped her eyes. His compelling presence caused her heart to beat faster, . . . so fast she could feel it fluttering against her chest.

Dirk drew in his breath sharply when he saw the flicker in the hollow of Shelley's throat. He raised his hand and gently touched the pulse beating there, for him.

She raised her eyes, eyes that were glowing, lids half closed.

"Shelley," he said in a harsh whisper.

She tore her gaze from his and tried to steady her breathing and slow the frantic beating of her heart. She brushed past him and headed for the garden gate, impervious to the riotous colors surrounding them.

Wordlessly, they claimed their bicycles and headed down Duval Street and around the block to Audubon House. By the time they entered, Shelley had her breath under control and had decided that earthshaking events like those could not happen again.

"This was another sea captain's house," Dirk was saying. "John James Audubon stayed with Captain Geiger while he was painting the wild life of the Florida Keys. I think you'll enjoy the film about the paintings done of local birds."

Shelley nodded without looking at Dirk.

The tension between them had eased somewhat as they mounted their bikes to continue up Whitehead toward home.

"There's no problem riding a bike here," Shelley said loudly enough for her voice to carry over to Dirk. "It's pleasantly level."

Dirk grinned. "You must see our hill. It has a 22-foot elevation. City cemetery on Margaret Street has a monument dedicated to the men killed on the U.S.S. Maine. Most of them are buried here."

"How sad, to be buried so far from home."

Dirk could only nod in agreement. After sailing along for another block, Shelley said, "I owe you an apology. I really thought you were joking about the Wrecker's License and the Rules. But I did love that tipped floor in the office."

"That was to keep that old wrecker, Captain Watlington, from missing the sea too much."

"Now show a little respect," Shelley scolded. "Remember, he was a Florida senator, too. Oh, look," Shelley broke off," there's the Courthouse." She ducked her head as she became aware of the apologetic glance Dirk sent her way.

To lighten the atmosphere between them, Dirk peddled over to a fence across the street. "And here's Hemingway's house. We passed this yesterday. They say there're forty cats living in this garden, all descendents of Hemingway's cats. It's too late today, but perhaps we can go tomorrow."

"I hope I'll be going home tomorrow," Shelley said quietly.

"Oh, yes. Of course. We should hear soon." He pointed across the street. "We passed that lighthouse, too. There's a military museum connected to it, but it'll also be closing in a few minutes. Another time for that, also. A spiral staircase inside the lighthouse takes you to the top. You'd have a wonderful view from there, including seeing the keys that stretch out to the south and west beyond our key. I wish you could stay for that, too."

"Another time."

As they neared the house, Dirk said, "Too bad the dog track closed last week. You might've enjoyed that."

"I don't think so. I know the rabbit isn't real, but I'm always afraid some dog might catch it," Shelley said as she walked Nuncie's bike around the house.

"You're just soft-hearted," Dirk teased.

Nuncie appeared in the doorway while they were rolling the bikes into the lean-to. "Dinner," she said.

"Bueno, Nuncie," Dirk said. "Give us ten minutes. We'll be right with you."

As they seated themselves, Nuncie brought in a beautiful white fluted tureen. The tempting aroma was almost more than Shelley could stand. "Nuncie," she pleaded, "what're you serving us that smells so good?"

"Una sopa," Nuncie answered, including a word Shelley was unable to understand.

"Perdóneme?"

"Como el pescado," Nuncie said as she passed a fragrant bowl of soup to Shelley, who turned to Dirk with raised eyebrows.

"Conch chowder," he translated.

"It's wonderful! Wonderful!" Shelley savored every mouthful. "I thought I wasn't hungry." She rolled her eyes before closing them, then ran the tip of her tongue over her lips.

Dirk had never thought of eating conch chowder as foreplay, but watching Shelley uninhibitedly experiencing the chowder gave him a jolt that had him imagining her responding to him in the same abandoned manner.

Swallowing heavily, he dragged himself back to the present. "It's my mother's recipe," he said with difficulty. "It's a family recipe, handed down." He shrugged. "They're like fingerprints. No two families make it the same way. In our family for instance, conch, which can be very tough, is tenderized by marinating it in lime juice. Most people pound it with the edge of a plate."

"Whatever happens to it, the result is heavenly," Shelley breathed as she savored another delicious mouthful.

After conch slices in marinara sauce ("oh, no, never too much conch," Shelley assured Nuncie) and Key lime pie, which Shelley was surprised to find almost white and not mint green in color, she went off to the living room to watch TV and Dirk went to the study to do background on a case.

Shelley was momentarily distracted by hearing a doorbell ring, but thinking it was on the TV program, she stayed where she was. In a few minutes Nuncie appeared at the door of the living room, a worried expression on her face and her hands clutched tightly across her apron.

Not understanding what Nuncie was saying, Shelley stepped into the hallway, surprised to see a woman standing inside the door. As Shelley approached, the woman turned and the light from the sconces illumined her face.

Shelley drew a sharp breath. Here? "Mother!" she exclaimed. "How did you get here?"

CHAPTER SEVEN

"Why, Michelle!" Her mother was equally astonished. "I flew, of course." She set her overnight case on the floor beside her and swept Shelley into her arms, murmuring, "Oh, my poor baby. What an ordeal you've been going through!"

"Mother, I'm fine. What I meant was how did you find me?"

"Oh, that. Well, I looked for Mr. Gentile's name in the telephone book. I found a Gentile with the same phone number you gave me. But it wouldn't have mattered. When I told the taxi driver where I wanted to go, he knew who lived here."

With resignation Shelley said, "Yes, I'm sure."

Turning to Nuncie, Shelley said, "Mom, this is Annunciata Jueves, Mr. Gentile's housekeeper. We call her Nuncie, and she's the world's best cook."

"Ah, yes, Señora Jueves. I am so pleased to meet you. Michelle has mentioned you several times."

Nuncie blushed as she answered, "Gracias, Señora."

"Thank you," Kate said with a slight nod of her head. "Michelle wouldn't have been in this situation if it weren't for me and my foolishness."

"Mother, you know I love you. It was my own foolishness that got me into this situation. I had the mistaken idea that getting the necklace back would solve everything. That's what got me into trouble.

"Perhaps, Michelle. But it was my request that sent you on this trip in the first place." Kate set her cup and saucer firmly on the table beside her.

Before Shelley could answer, Dirk interrupted, "I'll call Judge Haley in the morning and see if he can fit us into his schedule. I'm sure as soon as he meets you, and hears what you have to say, Shelley'll be on her way home."

In his heart of hearts, Dirk knew that was not what he wanted to happen. He wanted Shelley to stay here, with him, forever. He could teach her to love him, if he had enough time.

Kate watched him as his gaze held Shelley's. And was equally surprised at the intensity of Shelley's regard of him.

Feigning a yawn, Kate said, "I think I must be tired."

"Oh, mother. Of course you are. I don't know why I didn't think of that."

"Nuncie has put your case in the room next to Shelley's," Dirk said.

"Thanks, Dirk. C'mon, Mom. Let's go get comfy. 'Night, Dirk."

"Good night, Dirk. The coffee and cake were just what I needed. We'll see you in the morning."

"Good night. Sleep well. Don't rush to get up in the morning. I won't be able to call the judge at the Courthouse until after nine o'clock," Dirk warned.

Watching them climb the stairs, arms around each other's waist, Dirk could not help noticing how much they resembled one another: the same build, almost the same blonde hair, even the same way of walking. Making his way back to the library, he felt doubly guilty about the phone calls he was planning to make . . . but not guilty enough to change his plans.

After putting on their nighties and making themselves comfortable, the women settled in Shelley's room for a talk. If Kate was surprised at Shelley's choice of robe, she didn't comment.

"Mom," Shelley began, "you shouldn't have come down. I'm sure they'll get through to Tallahassee in the morning. I'll probably be home tomorrow night."

Brushing Shelley's comments aside with a wave of her hand, Kate pronounced, "I'm going to tell Frank everything."

"Do you really think you should, Mom?" Shelley asked. "Can't it wait a few more days?"

"No. Frank trusts me. I'm going to have to tell him the truth. Although what he'll think about your involvement, I can't imagine. He couldn't love you more if you were his own."

"I know, Mother. He's a sweet man."

"He's a very kind man," Kate said simply. "I'm sure he'll understand. If he doesn't, well, we'll just have to work it out."

Shelley patted her mother's hand. "I'm sure everything will be fine. Mr. Donovan'll be back shortly and this business with the necklace will be cleared up in no time."

"Let's hope, dear. Let's hope." With a change of subject, Kate continued, "What do you know about Mr. Gentile, Michelle?"

"Dirk Gentile? Other than he's Mr. Donovan's lawyer, not much. His family appears to've been here for years and he knows and is known by most of the people here on Key West."

"Yes, the taxi driver did know him," Kate said thoughtfully. "But I mean what sort of person is he?"

"I don't know, really. The police chief went to school and worked with Dirk's father, and another officer went to school with Dirk . . . . I really don't know much at all. But everybody here knows everybody else." After bringing her feet up and crossing them under her as she sat in the chair, she continued, "You might find this difficult to believe, Mom, but the judge went to school with Frank's brother, and with Dirk's mother! Probably Frank and Uncle Walt will know more about Dirk Gentile than we could ever find out."

Kate was quiet for a few minutes, eyes fixed on the distant wall. Bringing her eyes back to Shelley, she asked, "Did you see that picture of Dirk and that swarthy-complected man in the library?"

Shelley shook her head.

"It was on the table. They had their arms around each other's shoulders. They looked very chummy," Kate continued.

"Perhaps a relative?" Shelley suggested.

"Dirk's skin is tanned. That man looked very Spanish." With a seeming change of subject, Kate asked, "How far is it to Cuba?"

"About 90 miles." Shelley was beginning to zero in on her mother's train of thought.

"Mm-huh!" Kate said, leaning forward. "And how far to Central America?"

"I have no idea, Mom, but it's clear the other side of Cuba," Shelley answered, completely forgetting her own suspicions the day Dirk and she had been out on the "Double or Nothing". "Mother," she said firmly, "I don't believe Dirk's involved in anything illegal."

"Oh," said Kate. Then she brightened considerably. "But you don't know for sure?"

"Mom, I'm quite sure Dirk's an honorable man." Inside, she was having a struggle to forget his charges of trespassing. "What do you say we go to bed? You have a big day ahead of you, and I hope I do, too."

Meanwhile, downstairs, the 'honorable man' was finishing up the last of his phone calls.

"Hi Dad. Have you been enjoying your stay in Miami? . . . Uh-huh . . . You still planning to fly in early tomorrow? . . . Sure . . . . Miguel will crew. But, Dad, I won't be able to make it . . . . Oh, yeah, Hollis is counting on it . . . You know, Enos doesn't have anything on the docket tomorrow. Why not give him a call . . . Well, you know how it goes . . . Yeah, right! . . . Have a great time. Say hello to Mom for me and give her a kiss . . . Right! You, too."

The next morning, Kate and Shelley, dressed to appear in court, were at the breakfast table. The sun was shining in and birds were twittering in the trees when Dirk came out on the porch. He looked quite disturbed.

"Mrs. Wilson," he began . . . .

"Kate," she said. "Call me Kate."

"Thank you, Kate," he nodded. He continued with a slight pause, "Kate, I'm afraid your trip was in vain. Judge Haley's not in the Courthouse today."

"Not in the Courthouse? I thought he was the judge on duty this week!" Shelley exclaimed.

"You're correct, Shelley. He was. In fact, he is. But when I asked his aide about it, he said the docket was clear, so Judge Haley took the day off."

"Can't you get in touch with him?" Kate asked.

"I'm afraid not." Dirk shook his head. "He's gone deep-sea fishing."

Shelley slumped back in her chair. "Oh, my." Turning to her mother, she said, "I'm so sorry you came all this way, Mom."

"Don't worry about it, dear. It's just one of those things." Kate had been staring at Dirk, who shifted uneasily in his chair.

Nuncie came bustling in to put dishes of cool, colorful fruit in front of them. Shelley and Dirk picked up their spoons to begin savoring it. Kate gave Dirk a sharp, penetrating look, absently picking up her spoon while taking in the flush on his prominent cheekbones.

"Dirk, will Michelle have a police record?" she asked after a moment.

Dirk raised his head with a start. Somehow that was not what he thought Kate was going to ask him. Talk about a guilty conscience! "No," he managed after swallowing a mouthful of fruit. "When her clearance comes through, the charges will be dropped. It's too bad Judge Haley wasn't able to see you. Even though you're a close relative, he probably would've accepted your word as a character reference."

Kate was watching Dirk closely. Where was the open young man she met last night? Why wasn't he meeting her eyes?

"Sometimes the record remains on the police blotter even after the charges have been dropped," she pursued. "Will that happen to Michelle?"

"Some states have 'expungement laws', which provide for the erasure of police records of certain offences, or under certain conditions. I'll set things in motion to have that taken care of, as soon as she's cleared." Dirk felt a little uneasy for having omitted the fact that, so far, Florida was not one of the states to have an expungement law. And he felt he should not mention that a letter to the state's Attorney General was necessary to set the process in motion.

What he did say was, "Judge Haley has already decided Shelley didn't have 'criminal intent'."

"Well, I should hope not," Kate said in a horrified voice.

After calming down and staring at Dirk for a moment longer, she said, "I don't suppose you can give me the necklace and accept a check instead?"

"No, ma'am. I'd like to, believe me," Dirk said, sounding very sincere. "Judge Haley stated the giving of the necklace amounted to a verbal agreement between you and Mr. Donovan. We'd need Hugh's permission to release the necklace."

With a deep sigh, Kate shook her head. "This was a difficult way to learn several formidable lessons."

Dirk gazed at Shelley, a soft smile on his lips, a tender look in his eyes. "Shelley and I would never have met," he said quietly.

Shelley raised her head, shooting a glance at Dirk, then dropped her eyes in bewilderment. That man had done nothing but confuse her since the first moment they met. No, the second moment, she corrected herself. She could almost believe he did love her but, my word, he did have strange ways of showing it!

Kate noticed the look on Dirk's face and the becoming blush on Shelley's cheeks. It appeared she had been missing something, but what? She mentally shrugged. She knew Michelle would tell her in her own good time.

"My bag's at the foot of the stairs, Michelle. I'll call a taxi and go to the airport. Perhaps I can catch an earlier flight."

"Good idea, mom, but I'll drive you."

Dirk straightened in his chair, giving Shelley a frigid look.

"Dirk," Shelley said quietly, "I'm not going to run away. I want everything settled before I go. I don't want any more problems."

He flushed again. "Of course, Shelley. Take your time."

As Dirk walked into the study from waving Kate off, the telephone was ringing.

"Hello? . . . Oh, yes, Marietta . . . Yes, I hope they each catch a marlin apiece . . . I'm glad the Judge was excited about it . . . . Oh, yes, P.C.Universal . . . Free to go? . . . Yes, I guess she will be pleased to hear the news . . . . Um-hm. Thank you. Good-bye."

As Shelley reentered the house, Dirk was leaving the library. "Did your mother get off all right? Any problems?" he asked.

"Everything went very well. She got on an 11:00 o'clock flight and they were able to get her an earlier flight to Orlando."

"You and Kate are very close, aren't you?"

At Shelley's nod, he continued, "I suspected as much when you traveled this distance to help her out of her jam. But when she flew down to help you beat the trespassing charges . . . ." He shook his head.

"Yes, we are close, but no more than most families, I'm sure." she smiled. "That stuff about blood being thicker than water, it's probably true. Most families would rally around in time of trouble."

"Not necessarily. Come on into the library, Shelley, and sit down."

Dirk crossed to one of the wing chairs by the tall front windows and gestured to Shelley to sit in the other one.

"In my work I often see families split apart in time of trouble. It's quite moving to find a love and trust like that between you and your mother."

Shelley's amber eyes filled with tears. Dirk had hit a tender spot when he commented on their closeness. In her present anxious state, she was already close to the edge. It had been quite a wrench to see her mother's plane take off, especially since she had to remain in Key West. A surge of homesickness hit her and the captive tears rolled down her cheeks.

Dirk came out of his chair and knelt beside her, reaching out to hold her close to him. "Shelley, love, don't cry," he murmured. "Why are you upset?"

She turned her face into his shoulder. "I'm sorry. I'm not a crier. Not usually. I feel so frustrated!" She rubbed the tears away with the heel of her hand and took a big sniff. "Seeing my mother leave today made me realize all over again that I want to go home. Plus the not knowing when I'm going to find out that I can leave." She gave another sniff. "I'm homesick, too, I guess."

Dirk pressed her head against his shoulder and closed his eyes in anguish. He knew he was being selfish. He should tell her she was free to go, but he could not bring himself to do it. Swallowing hard, he said in a strangled voice, "Soon, love. You'll hear soon, I'm certain."

He patted her back and stroked her shoulder in a soothing manner. "I'm sure we'll hear tomorrow or the next day. They should have the storm damage cleaned up in the next few days." He stood and raised Shelley with him. Ignoring the startled look in her rain washed eyes, he seated himself in her chair and settled her in his lap, securely wrapped in his warm and muscular arms, her head tucked under his chin.

Shelley sighed deeply and cuddled closer, her arms sliding around Dirk's masculine ribs.

They sat there quietly, Dirk refusing to think of Shelley's predicament, content to hold her in his arms, her hair like satin against his throat.

Strangely, she was no longer homesick. She, too, was filled with contentment, feeling at home cradled in those powerful arms, being comforted by Dirk's nearness, and breathing in his own special spicy scent. It felt so natural to be in his arms. Was it true . . . that thing about captives falling in love with their captors? Was this feeling due to proximity . . . or was it something stronger? Whatever it was, it felt wonderful. She could probably spend the next year or so, right here in Dirk's arms.

She sighed drowsily and relaxed against him. His soothing strokes on her back and the tender massaging of the tense muscles in her shoulders hushed her the way a lullaby would.

Memories of the kiss they had shared Sunday evening burned through Dirk's mind. Gently moving her into the crook of his arm, he gazed down at her. She smiled up at him dreamily. Leaning down, he placed tender little kisses on her forehead and her winged eyebrows, then closed her eyes with melting touches.

She moved restlessly under his caresses, stretching to draw nearer to him.

Dirk's breathing accelerated as he by-passed Shelley's lips to place scorching kisses along her neck. Cradling her head in his strong hand, he arched her closer to his hungry mouth.

She opened amber eyes, soft and luminous, aroused with passion, as she became aware of the warmth of his body and of being surrounded by the enticing scent that was all his own. She found her arms moving upwards. Her hands slid sensuously over the rippling strength of his biceps and came to rest on his magnificent shoulders.

He groaned as her caresses brought her closer to him, her soft breasts pressed intimately against his strong chest. She fascinated him. He was obsessed with her. His mouth settled on hers as a hawk drops on its prey . . . sudden . . . intent.

His arms tightened around her. He loved her so. He had never felt this way about another woman. She had to love him! He would teach her to love him! She would forgive him for not letting her leave when she knew his reasons. And then she'd never leave him. They'd be together forever.

Nuncie's appearance at the door of the library broke into Dirk's dreams with the suddenness of an alarm clock announcing morning. And to Dirk, she was equally as welcome.

Shelley sprang to her feet, cheeks flushed, brushing at her skirt to cover her embarrassment. What was the matter with her that she forgot herself so completely in his arms? This had never happened with Rob! What is this strange power Dirk had over her? How could he make her forget that he was keeping her here on a barely acceptable charge?

Nuncie's cheeks were tinged with pink as she looked over Dirk's head and announced, "El almuerzo, Señor Dirk." She turned to leave.

Rising he said, "Gracias, Nuncie. We'll be right there."

Dirk reached for Shelley. She backed away from him, saying, "No, Dirk. This can't happen again. This isn't a normal situation and we mustn't treat it as such."

He dropped his hands in frustration. Things were not going the way he wanted them to. But then he brightened. His lawyer's logic came to the fore. She had said they must not treat this as a normal situation. It followed, therefore, that if this were a normal situation, it would be perfectly all right with her if he cuddled her on his lap and kissed her. She must be starting to love him after all!

Feeling much encouraged, he smiled and extended his hand. "Come, Shelley. Nuncie has lunch waiting for us."

Hesitantly, she put her hand in his and returned his smile . . . although hers wavered a bit.

As Dirk passed Shelley warm rolls to eat with her shrimp and avocado salad, he asked, "Have you ever considered working on the Gold Coast?"

"Gold Coast?"

"That area north of Miami." Dirk grinned. "It's a Mecca for the computer industry and many high-tech businesses. The Chamber of Commerce is jumping with joy over our new economic vitality." Then he laughed. "They've joked about naming it 'Megabyte Beach'."

"Move to Miami? No." She smiled in return. "I'm happy in Orlando working the way I do, using my modem or fax machine to stay in touch with Tallahassee. I have a lot of the benefits and none of the hassle." While she buttered her roll, she shook her head. "It would cost much more to live there.

Even if I had a sizeable increase in salary, I'd be no further ahead."

"Perhaps you could share a condo with someone," Dirk suggested, as he worked at scooping out his avocado and sneaked a peek at Shelley.

"No. I'm happy where I am. I'm buying a condo on one of the lakes. It's a lovely setting. Brilliant birds fly in among the flowering trees and bushes. Ducks and swans glide about on the lake. It's too beautiful a view to leave. Besides, I'm near Mom and Frank."

"Perhaps you'd want to share your condo?" Dirk asked, with a lifted eyebrow.

"Well, it does have two bedrooms," she said doubtfully, wondering where this line of questioning could be leading. "But I use one as my office.

"You'll have to get someone who'll share your bedroom."

Shelley stared at Dirk. Was he suggesting what she thought he was? Her heart lurched. She was mightily attracted to him, but share a bedroom? And in Orlando? What about Mom and Frank?

"Oh, no!" she answered breathlessly. "That would never work out."

"Not even if it were me?"

CHAPTER EIGHT

SHELLEY STARED AT DIRK IN wide-eyed amazement. "You?" she asked.

"Why are you so astonished?" he countered arrogantly. "You know I love you."

"I know what you've *said*. But I find it hard to believe. Your actions . . ." her voice faded as she stood and turned away from him. "What about Marilee? . . . . And what about Rob?"

"Shelley," he breathed, walking up behind her, "They don't matter. You and I are what matter." Placing his hands on her shoulders, he bent to kiss the silken skin below her ear. "I'm not serious about Marilee," he murmured. "She's a date when I need one, and that's the way she feels about me." He stroked her arms as he kissed a path around her ear. "You've dated Rob over a year, but you're not committed."

She stiffened, then closing her eyes, she bent her head to offer him easier access to her throat, all coherent thought leaving her. Groaning with pleasure almost too much to bear, he pulled her against his overheated body. As she melted against him, she sighed. Of their own volition his arms surrounded her, one around her waist, the other crossing her chest to allow his hand to slide lovingly over her rounded breast. Shelley trembled at his touch, feeling her breast tighten in response to his caresses. She was immobilized by the stunning pleasure coursing through her. She made no protest when Dirk turned her in his arms, pressing her intimately against him. Her arms curled upward, moving over his wonderful shoulders before sliding around his neck. She twined her fingers in his hair and nestled closer to his hard, masculine frame.

Dirk groaned again in rapture, feeling her body melt against his. It was the first time she had made a positive move toward him. His arms tightened in response and his mouth opened hungrily over hers. Feeling her mouth trembling beneath his, he moved his head for smoother access and slipped his searching tongue inside her receptive mouth. When Shelley pulled back to catch her breath, eyes dreamy, lips swollen and shiny from his marauding mouth, Dirk stared down at her, eyes darkened by pupils rimmed in silver.

"Oh, Shelley," he gasped, leaning his forehead against hers. Closing his eyes, he remained motionless, obviously trying to regain control. Slowly his arms loosened. Even more slowly, he withdrew from her. At her puzzled and hurt expression, he said softly, "My actions, remember? You said my actions don't show that I love you. Oh, yes," he whispered, "I love you all right. I hope I'm showing you by not taking advantage of you while you're in my custody."

Shelley's eyes glistened with tears. In spite of her tumultuous emotions, Dirk's explanation touched her deeply. She didn't know why she had responded to him the way she had. She had to allow that perhaps he was fond of her . . . all right, maybe he loved her, but this was no time to get involved. Perhaps when this fiasco was cleared up . . . .

She came out of her thoughts as Dirk gently touched her face, hearing him say, almost as an echo, "Perhaps when this fiasco is cleared up, we'll find each other again. Because I'm not giving you up, Shelley," he said in a fierce whisper. "Don't try to escape me!"

He dropped his hand, turned and walked to the screening near the gardenia bushes. Staring into the garden, he said, "I have to go out for a while. I have to check some records at City Hall for a probate I'm doing. I won't be too long." He jingled his keys in his pocket. "I won't ask you to come with me. I think we should be apart for a while." He smiled. "I probably wouldn't get anything accomplished with you sitting across from me in the Hall of Records."

Shelley wasn't too sure about that, but the more she thought of it, the more she agreed with Dirk. They had been together almost constantly. Space was what they needed.

Feeling a little lost after Dirk left, Shelley wandered into the library to look at the photograph her mother had mentioned.

Sticking her hands into the pockets of her lilac-sprigged sundress, she idly perused titles as she strolled past the book shelves. She was quite impressed by the variety of both the subject matter and the ages of some of the books. Bending over to see the lower shelves better, she backed up, bumping a typewriter case and setting it rocking. She grabbed it and straightened it before it could tip over.

Standing again, she drifted to the library table where a large framed photograph was displayed. Dirk and the dark-haired, swarthy-complected man, arms around each other's shoulders, laughed into the camera as if sharing the world's biggest joke. She started to smile in response when she picked up the photo.

She turned, smile still on her face, to see Nuncie, dust mop in hand, coming into the library.

"Quien es el hombre?" she asked Nuncie.

"Es su tio por el matrimonio. Es el esposo de la tia de Señor Dirk."

"Dirk's uncle," Shelley nodded. "Handsome man." She stepped aside as Nuncie ran the dust mop along the tiles at the edge of the beautiful carpet.

"El es un senador," Nuncie announced proudly, leaning on the handle of the mop. "Es mi primo hermano."

"Primo hermano?" Shelley repeated.

"Si. Es el hijo de mi tia."

"Ah, your cousin! Yes, of course. And a state senator! Your family must be very proud of him. Then you are Dirk's cousin?"

"No primo. Por el matrimonio solamente."

"Right! You are not related to Dirk. Your first cousin is married to Dirk's aunt. Got it!"

"Si. Si," Nuncie said with a big smile. She flicked the map toward the desk, lifting the typewriter case easily with one hand and setting it down silently. She gave the tiles a final flourish with the mop and pushed it ahead of her into the hall.

Shelley replaced the photograph, chuckling quietly to herself. His uncle—a state senator, no less! She could hardly wait to tell her mother. Kate and she had certainly been wrong about that sector of Dirk's life. Walking back toward the shelves she had been studying earlier, she cut the corner by the desk sharply and almost fell over the typewriter case. Shelley reached for it to set it upright again and was surprised by the weight, or rather the lack of weight. Come to think of it, it hadn't sounded 'heavy' when it went over. She remembered the weight of her portable typewriter, and while this case might have something in it, it certainly wasn't a typewriter!

She could feel whatever it was sliding around as she stood the case upright. Before she thought, Shelley had swung the case up on the desk and punched it open. A soft white cloth used as a wrapping was inside. She reached for it, opened it, and caught her breath at the jewelry lying there. The necklace was more beautiful for being displayed alone. And Frank had certainly been right—from the construction and design, this necklace had been an antique long before Elizabeth I had received it, and well before she had presented it to the first Lord in Frank Wilson's family.

Shelley, sighing with relief, rewrapped the necklace and replaced it in the case. She *knew* it had been in this room, but who would have dreamed . . . ? What did they say about hiding things in plain sight? Who in their right mind would expect anything but a typewriter to be in a portable's case, especially in the middle of a room? She gave another pleased sigh. She felt much better for knowing where it was, as though there were a bond between them, the necklace and herself. Yes, she really felt good about it. Naturally, there was no need to mention this to Dirk.

Shelley checked her watch. It was only about 2:30. Perhaps she'd walk into town to that little shop she'd seen down the street from the 'Captain's house'. She was getting heartily sick of her sundress. Maybe a pair of slacks and a top . . . she could always use them.

She called to Nuncie that she was going shopping and would be back in a bit. Shrugging when she received no answer, she walked out the door, down the path, and through the gate.

Though the afternoon was warm, a strong tropical breeze cooled the air. Being from Orlando, Shelley was not surprised by the profusion of colorful and fragrant flowers, but she was amazed by the towering subtropical palms and the huge shady banyan trees with their spreading branches and numerous trunks. Some of the Victorian houses, gingerbread trimmed, with striking 'lace work' in their porch railings, had broken with tradition and were sporting brave new San Francisco colors.

Shelley tried on several pairs of slacks and tops, but found herself walking out with a pair of coral jeans and a lighter colored coral top. She rationalized by telling herself the coral did wonderful things for her new tan.

Wandering along the street, she was drawn inside a store by some unusual jewelry. Amid the profusion of shell jewelry and trinkets, she found a necklace of gray, black, and white petaled flowers made of unglazed ceramic. Delightedly, she gave the young clerk her credit card. That necklace and some earrings to match had her mother's name written all over them. Kate would love them!

Dirk had not yet returned when Shelley had wandered back to the house. She changed into her new jeans and top and took a book out to the pleasantly shaded Florida room.

Not realizing she had dozed off, she was startled awake by the phone ringing next to her chair. After it had rung several times, and deciding Nuncie must be busy, she answered it.

After a pause the caller asked, "Is this the Gentile residence?"

"Yes, it is, but Mr. Gentile isn't home and Nuncie seems to be busy somewhere."

"Miss Morgan? Shelley?"

"Yes?"

"Aren't you . . . ? This is Hollis Mitchum. I thought you'd be . . . . When do you expect Dirk?"

"Anytime now. He went to City Hall to check some records. I got the impression he didn't expect to be gone long."

"Thank you. Ask him to call me, will you please? At home, if he misses me at headquarters."

"Sure, Hollis. How's everything with you?"

"Fine, Shelley. Ah, how is it . . . ?"

"I'm fine, too, Hollis. Disappointed at not hearing, but surely tomorrow."

There was a strangled sound at the other end of the phone before Hollis said, "Tell Dirk I need to speak with him. Have him call me, please. It's important."

"Of course, Hollis. Take care."

"Right. You, too. Good-bye, Shelley."

She sat with a frown between her eyebrows, staring at the phone wondering what it was that Hollis almost said, before she turned back to her book.

Hearing Dirk returning and calling for her, she answered him and flicked a look at her watch. She was astonished to see it was almost six o'clock.

"Sorry to be so long. It seems every few steps I met someone with a problem," he was saying as he stepped out on the screened porch. He stopped and drank in the sight of her.

He leaned down to put his hands on the arms of her chair and gaze into her eyes. His voice became low and husky. "I missed you. It felt as if part of me were missing. I hated to stop for those people. All I wanted was to get back to you." He placed a soft, quick kiss on Shelley's lips and then straightened. "You look good enough to eat."

"Oh, no," Shelley protested. "It's my new outfit. I went shopping while you were gone. Do you like it?"

"It makes you look as sweet as orange sherbet. You can wear it out to dinner tonight."

"Won't I need to wear a dress?" she asked doubtfully.

"No. Not on Key West. Informality is the rule. Even in restaurants that feature deluxe dining, you'll see T-shirts and shorts. I won't say people never dress up, but it's rare."

He threw himself into the wicker chair beside Shelley. "Would you like a cocktail? Or something else to drink? We have a great fruit juice concoction we mix with rum. I think you might like that."

"Fine, but easy on the rum. I usually just drink a little wine."

She walked to the kitchen door to watch Dirk mixing the drinks, admiring the interplay of his broad shoulder muscles beneath his gold knit shirt.

"Hollis called while you were gone. He seemed quite anxious for you to get in touch with him, even asked that you call him at home."

"Thanks, Shelley. I'll call him when I go up to change my shirt."

When Dirk was again seated by Shelley, the refreshing tinkle of ice cubes riding on the breeze, he turned to her. "I was serious about going out to dinner. This is Nuncie's afternoon and evening off. I'll name some restaurants and you make the choice. We could go to the Lighthouse Cafe on Duval Street. They have an outdoor terrace where they serve Southern Italian cooking, especially fresh seafood and pasta."

"Sounds good," Shelley offered.

"Now, wait," Dirk cautioned. "Another choice is Captain Bob's Shrimp Dock, a sort of family-style restaurant and, of course, it serves fresh seafood, too.

"That sounds nice."

"Then there's the Pier House. It's on the harbor in the old section of town. It's also in one of Key West's oldest buildings. It has a glass enclosed waterfront dining room, but I prefer the outdoor patio."

Shelley waited expectantly.

"Well, what do you think?" Dirk asked.

"You didn't mention the food at the Pier House."

"I didn't? Sorry. It's really great. We could look for 'the green flash'."

Shelley laughed delightedly. "It seems to me you've already made a choice. This is great with me! This is your territory, after all. But I don't know what you mean by the 'green flash'."

"Legend has it that if you're lucky, when the sun's setting you'll see a green flash just as the sun sinks below the horizon. It's very rare."

Shelley exhaled a soft breath. "Have you ever seen it?" she asked with widened eyes.

"Yes, I have. It's an exciting experience, a magical feeling. Most people collect at Old Mallory Square, the pier at the end of Duval Street. It has a sort of curious atmosphere. Jugglers, magicians, acrobats, and food sellers abound. But suddenly everyone turns to watch the sun set. A hush falls over the crowd and you feel you dare not blink, for fear you'll miss the flash."

Shelley drew another breath, eyes shining. "If you haven't already decided, may we go to the Pier House?" she asked.

Dirk laughed and squeezed her hand. "I hadn't decided, but I'll admit I loaded the information in its favor. In a town full of marvelous restaurants, it's my favorite."

After Shelley had brushed her hair and put on lipstick and Dirk had changed into a wine knit shirt that suited him even better than the gold, they set off hand in hand to walk the few blocks to the stop for the Conch Tour Train. Riding down Duval Street on the little seats of the open, blue-canopied cars, the breeze riffling through her hair and Dirk's arm around her . . . Shelley couldn't think of a place she'd rather be. Certainly not home in Orlando!

She became conscious of Dirk's voice, aware he had been speaking while she had been enjoying the warmth of his body next to hers and his strong arm resting on the back of the seat, hugging her close to him.

"I'm sorry. I didn't hear you."

"I was saying there's a state park on the end of the island off to our left."

"I can't see it," Shelley said, stretching her neck.

"It's really over several blocks." He chuckled as he squeezed her affectionately. "It's very beautiful in a rocky, rugged sort of way. Next to the park there's a naval installation that's a restricted area." He leaned down to check the street sign. "We're crossing Eaton Street. Over on the shore, about opposite here, is where Truman had his Little White House, his vacation home. It helped bring Key West back to the attention of the American people."

In the flurry of passengers leaving the Conch Train, all attempts at conversation were lost. Dirk put his arm around Shelley's waist to guide her through the exiting crowds. He almost had to carry her bodily from the fascinating sight of a fire eater. Two unicyclists juggling Indian clubs held her spellbound next. "Shelley, love," Dirk—said in her ear, "We have a reservation."

"Oh! Oh, sure." She gave several longing glances over her shoulder as they entered the Pier House. In the lobby, she stopped dead. "It's a hotel," she said almost accusingly.

"Yes, it is, but we're going out on the terrace of the restaurant. You'll be able to see the sunset from there."

The sweet-looking gray-haired hostess greeted Dirk with a kiss. "We haven't seen you here in a while, Dirk Edward. What's the occasion?"

"I'd like you to meet my guest from Orlando, Aunt Judith. This is Shelley Morgan.

"Nice to meet you, Shelley," Dirk's aunt said as she kissed her on the cheek. "How do you know Dirk Edward?"

Shelley flashed uncertain eyes at Dirk, breath catching in her throat.

"Shelley came down on business pertaining to some antique jewelry," he explained smoothly.

Shelley nodded in agreement. Aunt Judith's keen gray eyes narrowed as she glanced from one to the other.

"Isn't that a little out of your line, Dirk Edward? I thought you did corporate law."

"Sometimes things overlap, Auntie. In law, borders tend to blur occasionally," Dirk said philosophically.

"I saw your daddy earlier today," Dirk's aunt said over her shoulder as she led the way to the edge of the terrace. "He stopped in to tell me he got a sailfish. Said he's planning to have it mounted." She set the menus on the table. "Was telling me Enos got a tuna big enough to sell to the seafood place. Enjoy your dinner now. Stop, Dirk Edward, on your way out. Let me hear about your Momma."

Dirk seated Shelley, settled himself next to her and picked up his menu. Peering over it, he smiled sheepishly. "I didn't know she'd be here. She fills in for the regular hostess now and then." He looked at the menu again and cleared his throat. "She and Uncle Blair own this."

Shelley looked up from her menu, stared at him considering, smiled, nodded, and returned to her study. Finally, closing the huge card, she laid it aside. "You know what's best here. Why don't you order for both of us?"

"Fine with me. I love a chance to help you know my Key."

A fresh-faced young waitress with a long blonde braid down the back of her uniform came to take their order.

"Hi, Dirk Edward. What can I get you tonight?"

"Hi, Laura Jean. This is my friend from Orlando, Shelley Morgan. Laura Jean is a third cousin."

The two women smiled and nodded. "On his daddy's side," Laura Jean explained.

Shelley nodded again and dropped her eyes to where her hand was straightening the silverware, a small smile playing around her lips.

She heard Dirk say, "We'll have margueritas, and start dinner with the green turtle soup."

"The green turtle steak is good tonight."

At a smothered sound from Shelley, Dirk's lips twitched, but he continued seriously, "No. Bring us the snapper casserole and the shrimp broiled with wine and buttered crumbs. We'll probably share them."

"O.K. You want the fruit and yogurt or the tossed vegetable salad?"

In answer to Dirk's raised eyebrows, Shelley said, "Fruit, please."

"Thank you," Laura jean said in a lilting voice. "I'll get back to you."

"I get the impression that green turtle steak isn't your favorite food." Dirk smiled at her.

Shelley wrinkled her nose. "It's the idea, I guess. I've never eaten any."

"These turtles are specially raised for eating and are kept in turtle kraals over there not too far from where the shrimp boats dock," he said waving his hand toward the Gulf.

"I'll take your word for it," Shelley said, her nose still wrinkled.

The warmth of Dirk's fingers covering Shelley's radiated up her arm. She felt as if her blood were heating. She wished he would sit like a normal date, across the table, instead of so close to her. Not that she disliked it, exactly, but it did make her a little too warm.

"I think you'll like the shrimp dish. They're real Gulf crawfish. I know they'll be sweet, and tender enough to melt in your mouth." Dirk had picked her hand up while he was talking, holding it against his cheek, and absentmindedly kissing her fingers before curling them inside his hand.

Shelley found her breath trapped in her lungs. Although the sun was still well above the horizon, Dirk's eyes reflected the flickering glow of the candle on the table, snug in its hurricane globe. The intensity of his stare started her breathing again . . . and much too fast.

Food was served and removed, but they were more aware of each other. They talked . . . rather Dirk talked and Shelley listened, while he pointed out where the glass-bottomed boat was moored; extolled the virtues of the Key's snorkeling, scuba diving, sports fishing; mentioned that Key West had more than 100 points of interest to visit, until she begged him to stop, accusing him of being President of the Chamber of Commerce. He laughed with her, and confessed, "I guess I am overselling Key West to you, but I want you to love it as much as I do. I want you to look forward to spending time here."

She withdrew her hand. It had somehow found its way back into his comforting clasp. Straightening in her chair, she said quietly, "I'll be going home soon, Dirk."

"But surely you'll come back. I love you, Shelley. We're meant to be together . . ."

"Please, Dirk. We can't have a discussion about any of this until the charges against me are dropped and I'm free to go."

"But, Shelley . . . ."

"No, Dirk." She turned her face away, wondering if he would ever know what it cost her to stop him from telling her that they would be together.

In the ensuing tense silence, Laura Jean appeared. "Coffee? Key Lime Pie?"

Shelley shook her head. "No, thank you. Everything was wonderful"

"Even the turtle soup?"

"Even the turtle soup. It was delicious."

"But you're not ready for green turtle steak?"

"No, not yet."

"The check, please," Dirk murmured under cover of their laughter.

"The sun is setting, love. Watch for the green flash!"

Shelley sat entranced as the huge red disk, a strip of cloud across its face, sank slowly into the ocean.

"Now is when it happens," whispered Dirk as the last bit of red disappeared.

"Did you see it?" he asked, squeezing her hand.

"No, I didn't. Did you?"

"No, love, I didn't. I think there was too much haze. It happens most often on a bright clear evening. Well, this proves it. You'll have to come back to see it another time."

Shelley turned when they stood up to leave. A hush had fallen over the terrace; everyone had been watching the sunset, including the waitresses and busboys. She faced Dirk. "You weren't teasing, were you. It does happen."

"Yes, love. The green flash happens, and it's worth the long wait. It truly is a magical moment."

Outside the crowds were breaking up. Not too many people were boarding the little trains lined up at the Old Town Trolley Station. Most preferred to wander through the shops or bars, or to 'people watch'.

"Come." Dirk held his hand out to help her board. "Let's ride the Conch Train back to the house. It'll be a nice ride around the north side of the island and it's a lovely evening.

Shelley was in no hurry for the evening to end and fell in gladly with his plans.

He answered her question about the stick with the number on it. "A mile marker," he said. "Instead of naming an island or giving a street address when you ask directions, the residents give the mile marker. For instance, Islamorada is MM 84."

"There're a lot of interesting tales about the Keys," he continued. "Did you see that railroad bridge on your way down, the one that ended in the middle of a bay?

She shook her head. "It was too dark to see anything."

"Oh, right! Well, before that railway was built, the only way to Key West was by boat. People loved the railroad because it was faster and so picturesque. Much of it was over the water."

"What happened to it?" Shelley asked. "How did it break?"

"A couple of bad hurricanes hit just before the 1929 crash. They didn't have the money to rebuild. Besides, Route I was being pushed down the Keys by then."

"How sad. About the railroad, I mean." Shelley sat quietly for a minute. "I bet one of those hurricanes was the one that hit Key Largo. Remember, in that old movie, *Key Largo*, how they were all shut up in that old hotel during a hurricane. That was when I fell in love with Humphrey Bogart."

"Oh, yeah?' Dirk said in his best Bogie imitation. "Listen, sweetheart, I don't want you fallin' for any guy but me, see?"

"Dirk," she protested, snuggling up to him. "As if I could."

Had she just said what he thought she had? Dirk's heart leapt in his chest. "Shelley," he breathed, turning her in his arms. "My Shelley." His arms tightened around her, his eager lips unerringly finding hers in the dark. When they withdrew to

166

catch their breath, his eyes roamed over Shelley, his gentle fingers brushing back the golden tendrils the breezes had blown onto her cheeks, watching the light and shadows of the street lamps play across her face.

Occasionally the reflections of light on the Gulf would catch in the silver of his eyes. Shelley's emotions were frazzled, but she could see the depth of his love mirrored there. How could she continue to say 'no' when every nerve in her body was saying 'yes'?.

By now only a few people remained on the train. It had traveled around the north curve of the Key, past the brightly lighted motels, and was now headed through the quiet darkness along the Atlantic beaches, back toward the Gentile home. Never had 10 miles seemed to pass so swiftly,

Suddenly, Dirk tore his eyes from Shelley's. "Jerry," he called out. "Let us out here, will you, please?"

"Sure thing, Dirk ol-boy. Going sand walking, are ya?" Jerry asked as the little train coasted to a stop.

"Yeah, for a little while." He offered his hand to Shelley. "Thanks, Jerry."

The silence was wonderful after the Conch train had trundled off, the quiet swish of the waves adding a dream-like quality to the air. The moon rising from the sea intensified the sense of the surreal, its path of light reaching for the shore.

"Come with me, Shelley," he said, his voice low and husky. "Walk with me, love."

She put her hand trustingly into his. At that moment she would have gone anywhere with him, such was the magic of the night.

She stooped to remove her sandals. "No," he said. "Leave them on."

"Dirk!" she protested, struggling to stand erect in the powdery sand.

"Humor me, love. We'll be on the hard sand by the water in a minute."

A hair's breadth from the water, he stopped and took her in his arms. He bent his head and kissed her tenderly. "You're really mine now," he whispered. "There's a bewitching tale about this beach. The legend says if you get the sand of Southernmost Point in your shoes, you'll always return to Key West."

He drugged her with the intensity of his kisses. She made soft kitten-sounds in her throat, thankful he was holding her tight enough that her weak, trembling knees were not solely responsible for keeping her erect. It was like time out of mind. She could honestly believe she would return. She wanted to return . . . to Key West . . . and to Dirk.

Slowly, not breaking their kisses, he placed his arm beneath her knees and raised her to hold her close to his chest. Crunching across the sand, Shelley's arms around his powerful shoulders, Dirk was a man with a mission. She was his. And now he would show her how much he loved her.

He crossed the road and entered the yard, forcing the gate closed with his shoulder. He slid her along his heated body, touching her feet to the step as he unlocked the door. Pushing the door ajar, he bent to cover her lips with his, making a gentle foray into the moist darkness of her mouth, excited beyond belief by the purring sounds in Shelley's throat. Raising his head, he took a deep and steadying breath.

She leaned her head weakly against his chest. She could not tell whose was beating loudest. Never had she experienced such sensations as were vibrating within her.

Dirk moved them both inside, slammed the door, and automatically rearmed the alarm. He swept Shelley into his arms, taking the stairs two at a time. Outside her room, he once more stood her on her feet, kissing her passionately before opening the door and pushing her inside.

"Get into bed," he said, closing the door.

Shelley leaned against the wall. She felt as if she had been in a constant state of arousal since they had gone to dinner. How could he shut everything off like that? She walked unsteadily to the dressing table, where her trembling fingers removed her pearl studs from her ears. Staring into the mirror, she hardly recognized the slumberous-eyed woman with the flushed skin and the tousled hair. Self-consciously, she touched her kiss-swollen lips. Questioning her sanity at allowing such things to happen, she distractedly began to undress, knowing she would never sleep.

She hung her coral top in the closet and kicked off her sandals. She had unzipped her jeans and was sliding them down her hips when Dirk opened the door and walked in. Closing it behind him, he leaned against it. "You're not in bed," he said.

Shelley froze. "No," she whispered, not knowing if she were agreeing that she was not in bed, or if she were shocked by his overwhelming and exciting presence in her room.

"Good," he growled, walking toward her with the predatory stealth of his pirate ancestors. His short gray robe flipped open at every step, exposing his muscular thighs. Reaching her, he went down on one knee to help her finish removing her jeans. Tossing them on the chair, he stood and stared at her, gray eyes smoky with passion.

"If I'd known you were wearing that scrap of silk and lace," he said in a strangled voice, eyeing her peach teddy, "We'd have taken a taxi and been here an hour ago." He pulled her against him, eyes closed, and teeth gritted together. "Are you trying to drive me mad?"

Shelley melted into the heat of his body, her eyes closed, arms extended to smooth her hands over his magnificent shoulders, submerged in his musky scent. Feeling evidence of his blatant arousal, she started to pull away. "No," he shuddered, lowering his hands to her hips. "Stay here! Feel what you do to me!" He swallowed, striving to regain the control he was so close to losing. He bent his head, whispering against her lips, "I love you, Shelley. Let me show you. Let me show you how much I love you."

CHAPTER NINE

His mouth covered hers. The hand that had been restlessly gliding over her teddy slid relentlessly up to cover her tantalizing breast. Shelley breathed a ragged sigh into Dirk's mouth as her breast tightened and puckered in response.

"Oh, yes, my love. Yes," he groaned. Holding her close to his hips with one hand, the other slid the straps of the satin teddy over her shoulders. The sight of her breasts, tilted, taut, and ready for him, was the only thing that would cause him to release her hips. His hands hovered feverishly before grasping her gently around her ribs. He watched in fascination as his hands glided upwards to halt in a loving embrace around each eager breast.

Shelley arched in ecstasy, giving him better access. Her hands slid to his waist. Finding his belt, she loosened it. When she tried to push the robe from his shoulders, he shrugged it off and leaned down to kiss his way to where his hands had been.

She cried out when his lips closed over one of the peaks. Her breathing changed to sobbing gasps as he began to suck that heated tip. Her knees buckled as he switched to give the same loving treatment to her other breast. She barely felt him lift her and carry her to the bed. Not stopping to turn back the covers, he lowered her to the spread and followed her down.

He ran his tanned fingers through her tousled blonde hair before spreading it around her shoulders. Losing his hands in her hair, his mouth captured hers. He parted her lips and, stifling her little cries, he kissed her as he had dreamed of kissing her since he had first seen her.

His hair-covered chest rubbed sensuously over her aroused breasts. Leaning on his arms, his silver eyes darkened with passion and stared down into her slumberous amber ones. When he kissed his way along her heated and straining body, he slowly removed her teddy.

His kisses moved over her like a wave of fire, making her writhe in passion. She grasped his shoulders, murmuring incoherently.

He kissed his way along her bare and beautiful legs, moving the satin teddy over her feet and dropping it on the floor. She was so lovely. And she was his!

She was filled with a primitive excitement as he licked and nuzzled a path back to her swollen lips. En route, he lingered at her engorged and pouting breasts, driving her mad with impatience.

"Dirk," she moaned, moving her head restlessly on the spread. "Please, Dirk."

"My love." His voice cracked with emotion. "I've waited all my life for you."

At the juncture of her thighs, she could feel the way their passion was affecting him. Her hips raised in supplication.

He buried his head against her neck. "I can't wait much longer, love. I'm sorry."

"No, Dirk. Not 'sorry'," she whispered as she arched her spine again.

His weight pressed her into the mattress as his eyes blazed into hers. Heated flesh fused to heated flesh. She became conscious of his hand-dipping between their bodies and she arched again at that intimate caress. She felt she would die from the pleasure she was experiencing. She had wound her arms around him, holding him so close that they were as one but thinking to share the pleasure he had given her, she slid one hand down between their bodies and closed it over his heated velvet.

"Shelley," he groaned, "Don't. I have to be embraced by your sweet, warm body . . . to be one with you. Now!" he cried hoarsely, lowering his body to thrust into her satin sheath.

Never had she reached the heights and depths of passion that Dirk led her to. Never had he held such a warm and responsive woman in his arms. Her willingness to give to him challenged him to surpass any previous attempts at loving. Breathless and exhausted, they finally collapsed into sleep—arms, legs, and souls entwined.

Dirk awoke once, just before dawn, and found her eager and ready for him. Steamy and satisfied, he cuddled her against him, her head on his shoulder, his arm holding her close. He was filled with a tremendous energy and sleep was farthest from his mind. Lying there satiated, he relived the richest night of his life. All previous encounters were erased from his mind for he had found his mate, 'the eternal feminine', who was his alone.

Various solutions to their being together were revolving through his mind before the phone jingled on the nightstand next to him. Despite Dirk grabbing the phone on its first ring, it penetrated Shelley's sleep and she moved restlessly.

"Sh, baby. It's all right," Dirk soothed her. She smiled and turned over, snuggling beneath the covers.

"Yes?" he whispered into the phone.

"This is Hollis, Dirk. I called yesterday. I left word that it was imperative that I talk to you."

"Just a minute. I'm going to another phone," Dirk said in a low voice.

He laid the phone on the nightstand and left the room, closing the door softly behind him. He crossed the hallway to pick up the phone in his room. "Yes, Hollis. I got your message. I wasn't able to return your call last evening."

"Damn it, Dirk! Don't give me that! I called you yesterday because I was so pleased Shelley's clearance had come through while we were out on your boat. I know Marietta called you, because she knew we were all waiting for it. Imagine my surprise when Shelley answered your phone!"

In the other bedroom, the sound of the metallic voices disturbed Shelley's sleep. Recognizing Dirk's voice and hearing her name, she slid over into the warm area of the bed where Dirk had lain. Lying there, on the edge of sleep, the conversation started to make sense to her.

"Shelley's worried about her job," she heard Hollis say. "She's told you she has deadlines to meet. How'd you feel if she kept you from a court appearance?"

"Hollis, I can explain . . ."

"I don't think so, Dirk Edward. Bein' an only child, and bein' smart to boot, your Momma and your Daddy spoiled you rotten. But this is the most irresponsible thing you've ever done."

"Hollis, listen to me. I . . . I love her."

"Love her?" Hollis snorted. "What kind of love manipulates someone as sweet as that little lady?"

"I would've told her today," Dirk said impatiently.

"She's free to go, Dirk Edward!" Hollis stormed. "Let her go! Even if you can talk your way around your Momma, you could jeopardize your career. What you've done is against everything you've ever fought for or believed in. Your Daddy's so proud of you. What'll he say?"

"I'll explain it to them. Shelley loves me, too. She'll understand. So will they."

In the other room, Shelley was devastated. How could someone she believed to be as true blue, as straight arrow as Dirk do something so underhanded, and to her? He had said he loved her. And he had made love to her—not once, but twice. Hollis was right, Dirk was 'spoiled rotten!' He was arrogant and selfish. He was too controlling. Her wishes, her career, her *time*—all meaningless to him.

Hurt seared her lungs. She could barely breathe. Hearing the cessation of voices, she turned toward the window and pretended to be asleep. She felt as if she never wanted to see or talk to Dirk again. She could not bear to face him.

He walked in quietly and replaced the phone in its bracket. She heard the rustle of paper and then the door clicked shut. She lay quietly for the count of 60 before she opened her eyes. When she sat up, she found a note on Dirk's pillow.

"Shelley, my love,
I have to go out for a while.
I'm sorry. I wanted to be here
when you woke in my arms.
I love you.
D."

Shelley crumpled the note and threw it on the floor. What a fool she'd been! She had been so trusting! Her insides roiled with chagrin at the memory of how she had been tricked.

She climbed out of bed, showered quickly, and began to pack. Or as much packing as one could do, with a couple of plastic bags and the few things she had with her. It was time to wake up, in more ways than one. She pulled on her jeans and top, hands shaking, her insides churning with emotion. All his fine talk! The hurt was searing in its intensity, that he had taken advantage of her, but most of all, because she had responded so trustingly to him.

She picked up the tissue wrapped package holding the necklace she had bought for her mother. Holding it in her hand, she gazed unseeingly out the window. Her breath quickened. Of course! Frank's necklace!

She knew from the way Hugh Donovan had talked to her on Friday, that he would have let Dirk release the necklace to her. He had seemed such a reasonable and friendly man. He had known her mother would repay him.

Gathering her packages and purse, she crept stealthily down the stairs and into the library. Finding a sheet of paper and a pen in the middle drawer of the desk, she scratched out an I.O.U., opened the typewriter case, and made the exchange.

"Let's see how he feels when he opens the wrappings and finds that chit," she said, shoving the cloth-wrapped I.O.U. back into the case, slamming it, and replacing it beside the desk.

She wrapped Frank's antique necklace in tissue and placed it in the bottom of her largest plastic bag. The alarm device beside the front door was not blinking, so Shelley assumed, correctly, that the system had been disarmed. She walked out the door, down the path, and opened the wrought-iron gate. Getting into her car, she backed it out of the drive, and headed north. Not knowing where Dirk had gone, she also speculated that on the less traveled highway along the Atlantic, she was least likely to cross paths with him.

*　　*　　*　　*　　*

Escaping had been foremost in her mind and she had been barely conscious that the waving pampas grasses, growing around the salt ponds near the airport, would be one of her last sights of Key West. Even now the trials of her frantic journey up Route I had begun to fade. She gazed back along the Tamiami Trail. There was very little traffic, but she kept watching for a maroon Continental speeding after her. Could he have her arrested? Would he?

Sandwich forgotten in her hand, she brushed the tears from her eyes at the memory of Dirk's beautiful lovemaking—if it had been love. Her stomach clenched at the memory of his perfidy. Looking down and finding the half-eaten sandwich in her hand, she slowly rewrapped it.

Life goes on, she said to herself, mentally shrugging her shoulders. I need to get to Naples. I'll get some cash from an automated teller and find a motel off the main road. I'll have to play it by ear from there.

Staring off over the wild grasses of swamp, Shelley knew deep in her heart Dirk was searching for her. It seemed incredible that she had met him less than a week ago, but she felt a sense of inevitability. He had told her she was his and beneath the lawyer's civilized veneer pulsed the uncivilized blood of his pirate ancestors. But she had to try to escape! She had to, for her own peace of mind!

Naples was one of the wealthiest and most attractive cities on the west coast of Florida, its beautiful homes surrounded by lush flower gardens. One of its main attractions was the palm-shaded public beach that stretched for several miles along the Gulf Coast. In relief at reaching her goal in Old Naples, Shelley drove to one of the many avenues that dead end at the beach and parked her car at the side of the shady street. She walked through a charming gate and out onto the sand. She knew she had to think things through or Dirk Gentile would find her before she could get the necklace back to her mother.

She stood gazing at the waves slowly breaking on the shore. She was grateful for the soft shushing of the water and the whispering of the wind in the palms behind her. She sank down on the sand and let the peace and tranquility seep through her, soothing her after the emotionally tumultuous past twenty-four hours.

She tried to plan, but memories of Dirk's sensuous lovemaking intruded, causing concrete planning to be almost impossible. Tears streamed down her cheeks as she remembered his words of love and how cherished she had felt. Again feelings of betrayal filled her.

She sat huddled on the sand, staring seaward, as the memories took over. It was the first time she had allowed herself to cry and it had a purging effect. Eventually the tears ceased and the atmosphere of the peaceful area reached her again. With a shudder, she firmly closed the door on her memories, walked up the beach, and back to her car.

She spotted a branch of the Florida State Bank when she was driving through town. Parking the car in the lot, she used her bank card at the Automated Teller to withdraw some cash. That problem behind her, she set out to find a small and quiet motel.

The two-story motel that Shelley found about five o'clock was an older one, painted soft green and nestled among magnolias and other vividly flowering trees. Its welcoming atmosphere offered a haven to her, especially as it was off the beaten track.

She knew from past business trips that the license number and make of her car would be required when she registered. Sitting in her car across from the motel, she knew it would be a simple matter for Dirk to have Chief Hollis Mitchum ask his friends in the Florida State Police to trace her anywhere in the state. Now what could she do about that?

Glowering at the motel from where he was parked in the lot of the Holiday inn in Miami, Dirk waited the length of time he figured it would take Shelley to get there. Somehow he was not surprised when she failed to keep her reservation. Aggravated maybe, but not surprised.

With a growl, he picked up his car phone and called Key West Police Headquarters.

"Headquarters. Sergeant Greene."

"Dirk Gentile, Mitch. Let me talk to the chief, please."

"Sure thing, Dirk. Hold a minute, please."

"Chief Mitchum."

"Hollis, this is Dirk."

"Where you been, boy? I been tryin' to call you most of the day."

"You'll be glad to hear, Hollis, that Shelley's on her way home."

"Well, you finally got some sense. I knew your daddy didn't raise no dumb boy."

"Yeah, . . . Well, he might've. Hollis, I need your help. Ah, you see, Shelley and I had sort of a misunderstanding."

"Uh-huh. She found out and took off." Hollis chuckled in glee. "Good girl, that Shelley."

"Please, Hollis, I've got to find her. I've got to talk to her. I don't think she went home through Miami. Will you ask the State Police to be on the lookout for her red Volkswagen Cabriolet? And maybe check some motels that are stopping distance from Key West?"

"Dirk Edward, where are you?" Hollis asked in a provoked tone of voice.

"In Miami"

"Miami? No!"

"Yes, I'm in Miami."

"Oh, I believe you, boy. I just won't help you track down that poor put-upon little girl and let you continue harassing her. You kept her against her will. Even after she was free to go. So, contacting the State Police would definitely be against my better judgment. No, Dirk Edward. No."

There was a crushing silence before Dirk drew in a deep breath. "O.K., Hollis. Thanks anyway," he said, replacing the phone.

He went back to glowering at the motel. Tapping his fingers on the steering wheel, his mind churned in frustration.

Slamming the door of the Lincoln behind him, he strode into the lobby of the hotel. He fumed internally as a family of tourists registered and asked questions. Their two young children released their pent-up energy by racing around the sofa and love seats, nearly overturning the potted fig tree and other greenery located near them.

When finally they had gone off happily to their room, promising that everyone could swim before dinner, Dirk approached the desk. "I hope you can help me. I thought my fiancé, Shelley Morgan, was to meet me in this motel. I must have misunderstood." He gave a nervous laugh and ran his fingers through his hair. "Could you check by Telex and see where I'm supposed to be?"

The tall blonde could not imagine misplacing this Adonis with the sparkling gray eyes. She showed marvelous restraint, however. She merely smiled politely and asked, "Your name, please?"

"Of course," Dirk answered. He pulled a business card from his wallet and offered it to the woman behind the desk. The young lady's eyebrows arched as she read 'corporate law' and the prestigious office address. "Certainly, sir. Would you like to wait in the bar? It might take a little time."

"Thank you, no. I'll wait here in the lobby." Dirk said as he turned to pace restlessly.

Hailing a taxi, Shelley settled herself in the back seat after giving the name of the friendly-looking motel she had found. She congratulated herself on remembering the parking ramp she had passed on entering the city. Her little Cabriolet was tucked away on the fourth level, ready to be claimed in the morning.

Paying off the taxi, Shelley, carried her plastic bags to the registration desk. "I'd like a single room," she said to the elderly clerk. "I'll be paying cash."

"Yes, ma'am. Just fill out this registration." He slid the card across the desk and handed her a pen.

Registration! She wouldn't have to register the license number or make of her car, but she would have to register! She could not use her own name. She hadn't gone to all that trouble to hide her car to blow everything by using her real name. Making a lightening decision, she calmly reached for the pen, signed 'S. Mackensie', and firmly wrote the address of Frank's office in Orlando.

The clerk glanced over the form. "You didn't fill in your license number or the make of your car."

"I've come from the airport," Shelley said. "Please don't put any calls through to my room unless it's one from the airport.

How they could lose my luggage between here and Tampa . . ." She shook her head.

"That's easy," the friendly clerk said, leaning an elbow on the counter. "They never put 'em on the plane, that's how. Why, I could tell you stories—"

"Yes, I'm sure you could," Shelley said kindly. "Mr. Perkins, is it?" she asked, looking at the name plate on the desk.

"Yep. That's me. At your service."

"Mr. Perkins," she said in a low voice, "Someone will try to trace me. Please don't tell anyone I'm registered here." Under her breath, she said, "I couldn't stand it if he found me right now."

Mr. Perkins might have been elderly, but his hearing was excellent. "Poor little lady. Husband trouble, eh? Mean to you, was he?" His mustache bristled in indignation. "Never could stand a bully. Don't you worry your pretty little head. I won't put your name on the phone list. When the night man comes in, that's the one he'll check. You'll be safe, ma'am. You'll be safe."

'Husband trouble'! What a life saver! And she'd never said it. He'd just jumped to his own conclusions. Not correcting him, Shelley said, "Thank you, Mr. Perkins. I appreciate your understanding."

"No problem. No problem, ma'am." He cleared his throat noisily. "Well, there is one problem. As long as we don't have a credit card number for you, we have to ask for a deposit of twenty dollars to cover phone calls and other incidentals. You'd get it back in the morning," he said hastily.

"I have a phone company credit card. That would cover long distance calls. I might call my mother," Shelley said, mind working busily. "But, again, I might not. She warned me against him."

"Tsk, Tsk." Mr. Perkins shook his head, temporarily diverted from the question of the deposit. "Poor little thing. You need a good dinner. Nice place down a block and over one," he said, gesturing over his shoulder. "Run by a friend of mine. 'Anne's', it's called. Reasonable. Good food." He slid her key across the counter. "Settle in, then go for a hot meal."

"Thank you again, Mr. Perkins." Shelley smiled as she turned toward the stairs.

"Don't worry none," he called after her. "I won't let on you're here."

Shelley waved at him before turning to continue up the stairs.

Looking up, Dirk saw the blonde clerk at the desk signaling to him. The young lady's blue eyes roamed over him as he approached the counter, appreciating his muscular build and his masculine walk.

"I have good news and bad news, Mr. Gentile," she said.

At his quick and questioning glance, she put her fingers over her lips. "I'm sorry. I phrased that the wrong way. No joke intended, Sir. Miss Morgan does have a reservation here, but it's not guaranteed, and it's to be held only until six o'clock. It's 5:45 now," she said when he pushed back the cuff of his sleeve to check his watch.

"Yes," he agreed. He turned to stare toward the entrance, unconsciously rubbing the face of his watch.

"Our Telex doesn't show a reservation for her at our other hotels."

"Thank you," he said, belatedly remembering his manners.

"Sorry I couldn't be more helpful," the young lady said, thinking any woman would be a fool to keep him waiting.

"I really appreciate your help." Glancing around the lobby, he added thoughtfully, "I think I'll wait a few more minutes."

As an afterthought, he asked, "She didn't leave a message for me, did she?"

"I'll check, sir." She turned to look for a memo, wondering what kind of woman would treat this gorgeous hunk the way she had.

"No, Mr. Gentile. No messages," she said sorrowfully.

He nodded. "I'll wait."

When Shelley reached her room, she unpacked her sundress, hung it on a hanger on the back of the bathroom to help the wrinkles fall out, and headed into the shower. She leaned her head dejectedly against the wall while the hot water flowed over her, working magic on her tense muscles and tired body.

Turning off the water, she wrapped herself in a towel and went in to sit at the dainty French desk to use the phone.

"Hi, Mom. It's Shelley."

"Michelle, you're home. I'm so pleased. No matter how nice that handsome Dirk Gentile was, I'm glad to have you home."

"Yes. Well, I'm not exactly home, Mom," Shelley said. Right now, 'nice' was not the word she would use when thinking of Dirk. Then she winced at the shaft of pain that shot through her as she remembered the romantic moments on the beach at Southernmost Point.

Tamping the memories down, she continued, "Is Frank home yet?"

"No, not yet. Any time now. Where are you, Michelle?"

"I'm on my way home, Mother. I have the necklace. You won't have to worry about that anymore. You'll be able to put it back in Frank's safe deposit box."

"Dirk gave you the necklace? That's wonderful!"

"No, Mom, he didn't. I exchanged an I.O.U. for the necklace. You still have the problem of paying back the money."

"Yes, I know, dear. I decided while I was on Key West to tell Frank the whole story. I'll do that tonight. I have a nice dinner cooking and I have a fabulous wine breathing on the counter. I'm going to tell him after dinner."

"I think you're on the right track this time, Mom. Good for you!"

"We're going to have to talk about his traveling, too. Theoretically, he was retired when we married. Some retirement!"

"Frank loves you, Mom. You'll be able to work things out." Shelley leaned back in the small chair that accompanied the desk. "I'll be home by Sunday. But, mom, if Dirk calls you, please don't tell him you've heard from me."

"Why not, dear? He's such a lovely young man. And a lawyer."

"We'll talk about that when I get home, Mom. O.K.? Bye-bye."

"But, Michelle," her mother was saying when the telephone disconnected, "You didn't tell me where you are! . . . Drat!" she said, which was about as drastic as Kate got.

CHAPTER TEN

It was a muted click of the lock that allowed Dirk to enter his condominium on the top floor of one of Miami's new buildings. Letting the door swing closed behind him, he strolled over to stare out of the huge Palladian window that faced the ocean. He completely ignored the charm of the rest of the room: the Lawson sofa covered in a Native American design in wines, grays, and navy; the stained glass skylight, softly lit at night; the wood-beamed cathedral ceiling. He stood, lost in thought, absentmindedly jingling his keys in his pocket.

He had called Kate and Frank's number in Orlando, but no one had answered. He had left a message on Shelley's answering machine . . . twice! Finally he had called a friend of his, a private investigator in Orlando, to have him watch for Shelley's return to her condo. Now he had to wait.

In retrospect, he could see he had come on too strong, but he had never met a woman who had affected him the way Shelley had. What had possessed him to act in such an uncivilized manner?

He strode over to the French doors, slamming them open, and stamped to the edge of the terrace where he glared, unseeing, over the nighttime panorama. Grinding his teeth, he allowed Shelley might have had a reason to be angry. All right, she might have had several reasons! She had found out somehow. What had made him think he could escape her finding out he had lied to her? Well, maybe he had not lied, but certainly he had not been honest with her.

He had been living in a fool's world. All he wanted was to make her love him. The sweet way she had responded to him last night could only have been love. His loins tightened at the tender memories. Her skin was like satin . . . . He slammed his fist down against the railing. If he could only find her and convince her that he loved her and that he never wanted her to leave him.

He walked back inside to stand staring into the fireplace, his hand clinging to the mantle, his foot on the raised hearth disturbing the clay pots of cacti. Damn it, Hollis was right! He had acted irresponsibly. He had treated Shelley like a paper doll. He had ignored the fact that she had a life of her own and commitments to be met . . . . But she must know how much he loved her! Surely she would forgive him.

He turned angrily away, but the anger was directed at himself. Not since he had been a teenager had his hormones struggled so to overpower him. He groaned when he remembered that as a teenager he had shown more control than he had at thirty-three!

Hollis had every right to talk to him like a Dutch uncle. And Hollis was also right about his Dad—what would <u>he</u> think about his behavior?

Dirk became aware of the vivid slashes of color on the wall in front of him, slashes that slowly evolved into scenes of the Seminole Reservation not far from Miami. But tonight he derived no pleasure from these paintings. He could only continue to move restlessly around his apartment.

He missed Shelley.

Hah! That had to be the understatement of the year. He kicked at the ottoman as he prowled by. He stopped and stared at the telephone. He had done <u>one</u> more thing in an effort to track Shelley. He had called a buddy in the State Attorney's office. Through his influence, the State Police were now checking motels along the Tamiami Trail, or as they called it, 'Yew—S Route 41'.

It was after nine o'clock when the phone rang. It was Chuck telling him there had been no luck at the motels. Shelley's Cabriolet was not in any of the motel parking lots. There was also no record of a Michelle Morgan registered along the Tamiami Trail, up to and including Naples.

Dirk was in the process of disheartedly thanking him for his efforts when Chuck stopped him. "There is one thing, Dirk. One of the men, acting on a hunch, questioned the attendant at a parking garage in Naples. The man thought he remembered a small red convertible. When the officers cruised up the ramp, they found a car matching that description on the fourth level and it was carrying Orlando plates. I don't know what you want to do about it, but that's all they could come up with.'

"Chuck, I owe you one. No. This is a big one. I owe you <u>two</u>," Dirk said with a tremendous sigh. "Call in my marker whenever you need to. I'm really indebted to you."

Dirk's mind was clicking like a computer as he rode the elevator down to the parking area beneath his building. In a little over an hour and a half, he had traveled the 106 mile distance between the cities and was cruising the streets of Naples. He avoided the large, brightly-lighted motels and was searching out smaller ones. He wasn't going to fall for that one again.

It was late, after midnight, when Dirk happened upon the motel where Shelley was staying. Dirk gave the man his card and described Shelley. The clerk shook his head and showed Dirk the phone list.

"Mostly salesmen, Thursday nights," he volunteered. "Not many single ladies."

Dirk nodded his head. "I'd appreciate hearing from you if someone of Miss Morgan's description should show up." He looked at the desk clerk intently.

"We'll see what we can do." The man nodded back at Dirk.

Sure couldn't tell by looking, the desk clerk thought to himself. This man looked like an all-right guy. Just can't tell, it seems.

The desk clerk was brought out of his musings when Dirk started to leave, then turned back to the desk. "I'm exhausted," he said. "I've stopped at every small hotel in Naples. Do you happen to have a room for me?"

Having given Dirk the key to a room as far from Shelley's room as possible, and finally being relieved by the night clerk, Mr. Perkins went off to use the phone in the Housekeeping office. When Shelley drowsily answered her phone, he spoke in a very low voice. "Miss Mackensie, I think your husband's here."

"What?" Shelley squeaked in a strangled voice.

"It's me, Dan Perkins. A man came in just now. The night clerk was late so I was still on duty. Gave me his card. An attorney. Let me get it out here." Shelley held her breath as he fumbled for the card. "Yep. Here it is. 'Dirk E. Gentile', it says here. Tall dark-haired man. Gray eyes. Described you to a T."

At Shelley's gasp, he continued. "Now, don't you worry none, little lady. I showed him the phone list and, like we agreed, your name isn't on it."

"Mr. Perkins, how can I thank you? I do appreciate what you've done for me."

"Least I could do, ma'am. Least I could do. My daughter's man was mean to her. Enough said."

"Nevertheless, I do thank you," she said, but not without a niggling feeling of guilt at having given that dear man the wrong impression about Dirk.

"One big trouble, though. Mr. Gentile says he's stopped at all the other small motels." Mr. Perkins paused for a comment from Shelley.

"Yes?" she said encouragingly, wondering what was coming next.

"It seems he's tired, so he checked into a room here."

"Here?" Shelley choked over the word. "In this motel?"

"Yes ma'am. But don't you worry none. I put him in a room a good distance from yours. You take care now." Mr. Perkins hung up briskly.

"Thank you. You, too." Shelley said into the hollowness of the empty line.

She sat on the edge of the bed, all thought of sleep vanishing. She had to get out of there! What was the name of the taxi that had brought her to the motel? The yellow pages would have it!

Flipping rapidly through the phone book, she found the taxi number and called it, asking that she be picked up at the side entrance of the motel, the one nearest her room. Quickly dressing and thrusting everything into her plastic bags, she hurried down to wait at the entrance.

The taxi drew up, but before he could honk, Shelley opened the cab's back door and jumped in. Giving the address of the parking ramp where she had left her car, she settled back into the darkness of the back seat.

In his room at the other end of the building, Dirk turned over restlessly. He had been dreaming of Shelley. It had been so real. He could feel her near him. Yet the longer he thought of her, the farther away she seemed to be. Shaking his head, he punched up his pillow and settled back on it. Would it be like this forever? . . . Missing her the way he did, never seeming to get closer?

A woman with long blonde hair was riding up front with the driver of the cab, . . . evidently his girlfriend. Shelley noticed thankfully that he was much more interested in his friend than he was in his fare. Drawing up to the parking garage, the driver tucked the bills Shelley had thrust at him into his shirt pocket and drove off laughing and joking with the woman. This was one time Shelley was delighted to be ignored. She knew the driver would never be able to identify her.

It was with a feeling of relief that Shelley rode the elevator to the fourth level of the garage and unlocked her car. She congratulated herself on her choice of parking, especially for choosing a garage that was open 24 hours.

The night attendant eyed her red Cabriolet and gave her a searching look as he took her parking fee, but said nothing about the State Police checking her car. Shelley turned left and drove north to join I-75, knowing she would make better time on a superhighway.

After driving for about two hours, she turned onto US 301 just past Bradenton. She was desperately in need of a cup of coffee and an opportunity to stretch her neck and shoulder muscles. She knew a truck route would have restaurants and gas stations that were open all night.

Pulling into a diner, she entered and walked over to a booth near the front. The few truck drivers turned back to their coffee after perusing her with the admiring glances they would have given any attractive woman. She gave her order for black coffee and apple pie to the broad-shouldered, bearded man in an apron.

When he returned, he set the coffee and pie down slowly in front of her. He put a small cream container on the table when she finally raised her eyes to his.

"Any problems, Miss?" he asked kindly.

"No. No problems." She picked up her fork.

"Don't see many women traveling alone at night." He stood stolidly by the table.

Shelley thought quickly. "A family matter. I'm on my way home."

"Where is home?" he asked,

"Orlando," she answered, wondering at his line of questioning.

"The boys will keep an eye out for you." He jerked his head at the truckers seated at the big round table. "They worry about a woman traveling alone at night, too. That little Cabriolet out there yours?" At Shelley's hesitant "Yes", he nodded his head and returned to his seat behind the cash register, picking up his newspaper.

Shelley noticed he had a few quiet words for each of the drivers as they paid their checks. When they left, they cast discrete glances in Shelley's direction and nodded shyly.

"C.B.'s will be busy for a while," the counterman smiled as he accepted her money. "But they'll watch out for you."

"Thank you," Shelley said over the lump in her throat and turned away before he saw the glint of tears in her eyes.

Suddenly a thought struck her and she whirled back. "Won't the State Police hear what's said on a C.B.?"

"Yeah," the burly man nodded. "Sometimes." Seeing her distress, he continued, "it depends on how busy they are."

"Could you . . . could the C.B.'s not mention me, or my license number along the road?" Shelley nervously twisted the strap to her shoulder bag.

"The boys won't mention your license number, ma'am. More likely they'll give you a code name, like <u>Little Red</u>—for your car, you know."

"That's good to hear, but . . . but . . ."

"You do have a problem, don't you, Miss?" The bright blue eyes shone kindly from the bearded face. "You can trust us."

The straps on Shelley's bag came in for more punishment before she reached a decision. "There's a man looking for me," she said breathlessly. "He has friends . . . . I'd appreciate it if the fewest possible people knew where I am."

"He with the Mob? A drug dealer?" the man asked sharply.

"Oh, no," Shelley said, shaking her head and raising one hand in protest. "I just can't let him find me." The straps on her bag were twisted even more tightly. "He has a friend who's a policeman, a Chief, actually. I'm afraid he might try to track me through the State Police or something like that."

"Ahh," the man with the apron said. "Got it! I'll pass the word."

"Do you have a C.B. here?"

"No. There's a lull, now. None of the men in here. But drivers are in and out of here all the time. It'll be easy as pie to get the word out."

"Thank you. And thank the truck drivers, too, please."

As Shelley drove through the wisps of fog that held back the dawn, she found it difficult to believe less than a week had passed since her mother's startling request that Shelley retrieve Frank's necklace from Hugh Donovan. Who would have dreamed she would meet a man like Dirk Gentile . . . let alone make love with him! Tears filled her eyes at the memory of his seduction and betrayal. At the same time, heat spread through her system, out to her very nerve endings, at the memory of his magnificent body, his tender touches, and the unforgettable love they had shared.

The Cabriolet started to slow down. Love! Yes, she reflected, it had been love on her part. She could never have given herself so completely if she had not loved him. But what about Dirk? He had said he loved her but who knew what he had felt? And he had lied to her! She had been free to leave, heaven knew for how long! No wonder Hollis' conversation had been so disjointed.

If she ever saw Dirk again, could she trust him? Realizing the little red car was slowly drifting to the side of the road, she straightened it out and brought it up to speed. She was grateful that the freeway was almost deserted at that hour of the morning, except for the trucks that were rolling. The drive up 301 and over I-4 was almost without incident. A few times a truck had slowed down in front of her, another pulled in close behind, while a third 18-wheeler had pulled alongside. The first time it had happened, she was terrified. Her car was so small and they were so big! Her fears were quieted however, when she caught a glimpse of the flashing lights of a police car, stopped on the shoulder of the road, as she and her convoy swept by. The other times that had happened, she had felt protected, safe. She had never thought of guardian angels as traveling in 18-wheel Peterbuilts.

The sky was graying when she pulled into her parking space in Orlando. Shelley played the messages on her answering machine when she came into her condo. There were calls from friends for dates that had come and gone, and two frantic messages from Dirk demanding she call him, and giving her several numbers where he could be reached. Shelley cold-bloodedly pushed the erase button and went off to take a shower. After the relaxing shower, she went to bed, figuring two hours' sleep were better than none.

When she awoke, she dressed and called her friend Sandra in Tallahassee, asking if she could stay with her for a week. Sandy was delighted.

Shelley bundled up the projects she was working on and packed some clothes. Nothing coral colored in the lot, she noticed.

On her way out of town, she detoured by Kate's house. The sun was warming the orange blossoms and their sweet scent permeated the air. The breezes rippled over the surfaces of sparkling lakes sprinkled generously through the city's park like settings. Shelley hated to think of spending the next week in Tallahassee. Orlando was a simple, friendly city, . . . picturesque with a small town pace, quite a change from the bustling capitol.

It was already 10 o'clock and Frank had left for the day when Shelley rang Kate's doorbell. After the initial hugs and kisses came the assurances that it seemed longer than two days since they had seen each other.

After the excitement and trials of the past week, handing over the antique necklace was almost anticlimactic. In fact, its appearance was greeted quietly by Kate, tears glinting in her eyes. "I'll put this back in the safe deposit box as soon as I can. You can't know how much this means to me, Michelle."

"I think I can come close, Mother," Shelley answered in an equally quiet voice.

"Oh, my dear. Of course you can." Kate hugged Shelley to her. "Come over and sit on the sofa with me. Will you have some coffee?" At Shelley's nod, she busied herself with cups and the coffee pot. "Did you know Dirk Gentile called here this morning? He said he called last night, but it must have been when Frank and I'd gone for our walk."

"I suspected he'd call you. Mom, I'm going to stay with Sandy in Tallahassee for a few days. Please don't tell Dirk where I've gone."

"Why, Michelle, whatever happened?"

Shelley looked into her cup. "Let's just say Dirk and I did not part on the best of terms."

"I'm sorry, dear. I feel badly that Frank and I've achieved our happiness at the loss of yours. Because you did seem happy. Dirk's such a nice young man and he seemed quite smitten with you."

Shelley shrugged her shoulders and stared out the window. She knew if she tried to protest, she'd cry.

Kate bit her lip and decided to plunge ahead. "Frank and I had a wonderful talk. He understood completely how lonely I become when he travels. We really cleared the air. It was the best discussion we've had since we've been married."

"Mom, I'm so pleased for you. I knew Frank would understand.

"You know Frank pretty well, too." Kate looked down at her twisted fingers. "He decided his assistant could share more of the traveling. He's a charming young man and has a perfect background for the job." She gave a little smile. "If it's a job Frank has to cover himself, and he must be gone for several days, then he's going to take me with him."

"I knew you'd work things out, Mom. You love each other so much."

"Best of all, Michelle, Frank made an appointment for us to meet with Hugh Donovan on Monday to settle my debt. How foolish I was . . ." Kate's voice trailed away. "He was so wonderful." She spoke in a stronger voice. He said there was no question of stolen property. He said, 'What's mine is my wife's.' Isn't that remarkable? That's the way I'd always felt, but this upset over the necklace had me so mixed up. But I've always felt what little I have is Frank's," she continued with trembling lips.

She held a tissue to her mouth. "He also said an old necklace couldn't begin to be a trade for the way you and I have welcomed him into our family."

Tears sparkled on Shelley's lashes. "Oh, Mom."

"There's more," Kate said with a sniff. "He said, 'No monetary value could ever be placed on a sweet, loyal, and loving daughter like Shelley. Everything she became involved in came about because she tried to spare us any problems.' Isn't he wonderful?" Kate was openly wiping her eyes.

Shelley and Kate clung to each other until Kate gave a little laugh and pushed away. "How was your trip back? When did you get home?" she asked, as she blotted the area beneath her eyes with her tissue.

Shelley had long since decided the less said about her Key West trip the better it would be. She discretely ignored the question as she handed her mother the tissue-wrapped package she had brought back for her.

"This jumped off the counter and said, 'Take me to your mother'," Shelley laughed.

Kate unwrapped the tissue with childlike enthusiasm. "Shelley! it's exquisite, and handmade, too. The petals are perfect on the flowers. Who but you would know how I love gray and black with white!

"There're earrings, too," Shelley said, shaking the tissue.

"So there are. It's a beautiful set, Michelle. Thank you so much."

"De nada," she said in an off-hand manner. "They begged to be brought to you." She rose to her feet. "I'm off, Mom. I'm behind in a lot of my work and it'll be best to go into the office in Tallahassee. I'll probably be working tomorrow and Sunday, too, trying to get caught up. I'll call you when I get a chance. Remember, Mother, please don't tell Dirk Gentile where I've gone."

Shelley had scarcely made it to her car, when Kate's phone rang. She paused in the act of putting on her coat to stand staring at the phone, a small frown between her eyes. After it had rung six times, Kate knew the caller was not going to give up. Walking slowly toward the telephone, she also had a premonition of who was calling. She picked up the phone, but before she could answer, she heard Dirk Gentile's voice.

"Kate? . . . Mrs. Wilson?."

"We decided on Kate, remember?"

"Yes, Kate. Ah, I'm still trying to locate Shelley. I'm afraid she might've had some trouble on the road. Have you heard from her?"

"Shelley came home. There's no problem there."

"You've talked to Shelley?"

"Yes."

"What did she say, about anything, I mean?" Dirk held his breath for Kate's answer.

"She wouldn't talk about . . . anything."

"I must get in touch with her. Please tell me how I can." Dirk wiped the perspiration from his forehead, as he paced back and forth.

"I can't do that, Dirk. I'm sorry. I'll tell her you called when I speak to her. Does she know how to get in touch with you?"

"I left some numbers where she can get in touch with me, but I'll give them to you, too. If you don't mind taking them?"

"No, of course not. Fire away." Kate wrote rapidly for several minutes. "Got 'em."

Dirk was quiet for a minute. "Do you think it'll do any good if I come up there to Orlando?"

"No, Dirk, I don't. I can tell you this, Shelley is not in Orlando. That's all I can tell you, but it'll save you a trip."

"Thank you, Kate. And thank you for talking to me. Please tell her I called and ask her to give me a chance to explain. Kate, I do love her," Dirk's voice broke.

Kate choked up in response. "I know, Dirk. Why else would you've given her the necklace? Good-bye, now."

'Given her the necklace'? Dirk stood staring over the Miami skyline. 'Necklace'?

On sudden impulse, he called his home in Key West.

"Nuncie, where are you?" Dirk shouted as Nuncie had barely picked up the telephone.

"Aqui! Señor Dirk. Aqui!"

"Are you in the library?"

"No, Señor Dirk. Yo . . ."

"Go into the library and pick up the phone on the desk."

"Si. Si."

After a pause, Nuncie picked up the phone. "Si, Señor Dirk?"

"There's a typewriter case on the floor by the desk. Get it. Put it on the desk and open it," Dirk ordered with machine gun delivery.

After much clicking and snapping, Nuncie packed up the phone. "Si, eet is open."

"Look inside, please. Tell me what's inside."

"Algo de material y una nota."

"No necklace? No jewelry?"

"No, Señor Dirk. Solamente el material y una nota."

"Gracias, Annunciata. I'm sorry for shouting at you," he continued in Spanish. "I was a little upset."

"De nada, Señor Dirk. No problema."

"Gracias, Nuncie. Adios."

As Dirk sat with his hand on the phone, he suddenly started to laugh. "That little devil! She got even with me," he chuckled. "And she got what she came for! I'll never figure out how her mind works, but what wonderful fun we'll have while I try. And what a wonderful excuse I have to look for her."

CHAPTER ELEVEN

SANDY ANSWERED THE DOOR WITH a big smile and drew Shelley inside, chattering all the while. The tropical storm, trouble with the electricity, how inconvenient to be without a phone, the problems with the heavy rains, the storm damage . . . all were covered, non-stop. "Everybody'll be working this weekend. Yesterday and today were fairly normal," Sandy was saying as she dove into the closet to retrieve a hanger from the floor. "The deadline's Wednesday, as you well know," she continued as she hung up Shelley's jacket.

"Come over here and have some coffee. I made it when I got home. I figured you'd be here about now." Sandy poured coffee and handed it to Shelley before she had a chance to settle herself. "Tell me, what were you doing on Key West?" Sandy finally paused and looked expectantly at Shelley.

"How . . . how did you know I was in Key West?" Shelley asked dazedly.

"Oh, that's easy." Sandy waved one hand breezily. "When you called in asking for time off for personal business, and nobody here knew what that business was, well—" she shrugged her shoulders, "I just called your mom on Sunday."

"What did she tell you?"

"She said you had business with a lawyer in Key West and you'd run into a series of delays."

Shelley nodded sagely while her insides leapt at what must have been the understatement of the year. "Yes, it was one frustration after another. It's a good thing I called the office last Friday before I left. Not being able to reach it earlier this week was at the top of my frustration list."

"Tell me about it! It took me until Wednesday afternoon to get your mother." Sandy leaned forward from where she sat close-legged on the floor on the opposite side of the coffee table. "Did you hear about Jim Bouchard? You know how he leaves his computer open all the time, even on weekends? The storm blew out his monitor and fried the motherboard! Wow! Was Jerry teed off! Working from home the way you do, you miss a lot of the inside stuff, but I can't tell you how many times Jerry has yammered at Tim about that. Well, what would you like to do about dinner?" Sandra's voice scampered on. "Chinese? Mexican? Seafood?"

Chinese was decided on and Shelley unpacked in the guest room while Sandy called for a reservation. It was a quiet dinner.

Both women were 'Friday-night-tired' and, with a weekend of work staring at them, decided on an early night.

Although Shelley's time at the main office of *Strategic Computing* magazine was limited to phone calls, faxes, modem exchanges, and a personal visit for meetings once a month, she had made quite a few friends. She smilingly made her way through the flurry of surprised greetings to the cubicle she called her own in Tallahassee. She settled down with a contented sigh. The soft clicks of the computer keys, the background hum of the computers, and the whirring of the laser printers blending with the murmur of voices in the cubicles around her, gave her a feeling of normality after a very trying week—a sort of business-as-usual feeling that was very soothing. She was even accepting of the hideous and unflattering fluorescent lighting.

When she turned on her computer and the programs began downloading, she checked the correspondence that had been held in the office for her. Naturally one or two letters picked her reports and articles apart, but the majority was favorable and several offered ideas for future articles. She set those aside for the next editorial planning meeting.

She had begun unpacking her briefcase and setting out the products she was planning to review for the next issue when her phone rang. She stared at it for two more rings, heart pounding.

Sandy appeared in the doorway at the fourth ring. "Oops! Sorry. Thought you'd gone somewhere. I was going to get the phone."

"Thanks, Sandy. I've got it," Shelley said as she steeled herself to pick up the receiver. "Hello?" she said tentatively.

"Sorry if I disturbed you when you were busy," Jerry's voice came over the line. "Could you come into my office please?"

"You bet." Shelley's voice sounded positively carefree. "Five minutes be O.K.?"

"Great. Bring your calendar."

Shelley hung up, clasped her hands in her lap and bowed her head. She had been so afraid it would be Dirk on the line . . . although how he would have found her . . . . Yet she had dialed this office several times from his home, trying to get through. There would have been no problem securing the number from the business office of the telephone company, even if he did not know the name of the magazine. After all, it was his phone and the number probably had been electronically recorded. But . . . and this was something to wonder about, was a number recorded if the call was uncompleted?

She raised her head, heaved a huge sigh, gave a Scarlett O'Hara shrug, and picked up her appointment diary. She gave a half-hearted brush at her gray skirt and straightened her sweater with the Indian design on it. Her gray leather pumps made no noise on the rust carpeting that led to Jerry's office.

At her soft tap at the door leading into his office, Jerry looked up and smiled. "Come in. Sit down. How was your business resolved?"

"Satisfactorily. Mom is happy; Frank is happy,—so I'm happy."

"Good! Good!" he nodded.

Shelly had a feeling he would have reacted the same way if she had told him she'd spent those four days in Dirk's custody.

Jerry got right down to it. "We're really strung out. Those two and a half days of down time really put it to us. As you know, one of the primary focuses of your job is to keep track of what's going on in the industry and decide how to treat it. There's a trade show in Orlando this coming week that we're involved in. Cathy's supposed to moderate a panel discussion. You did an article,—what—, two issues ago,—on copyright abuse?"

"I think the slant was the protection of copyrighted programs," Shelley murmured.

"Right! Right! The panel discussion's going to cover suggestions for the prevention of copyright infringements, what can be done about pirating programs, and so on."

Shelley nodded in response to his nod, and raised her eyebrows to show she was with him.

"Call ExperTech. Talk to the president. They've developed a security program that can immediately blank the screen when unauthorized personnel enter the area. Only the operator's personal password can provide reentry. Their president was telling me the licensing is one disk per machine, so how can a 10-PC office operate with purchasing only one program? See what she says."

"Sure. Anything else?" She looked up from making notes in her calendar. "I'm sorry. I didn't hear you." At least she hoped she had not heard him.

"I said, 'I want you to moderate the panel'."

"But Cathy's lined up," Shelley protested.

"Cathy has to go to Texas to cover an explosive follow-up of an article in the last issue of a rival magazine. She'd done a similar article, a much fairer slant, and the company's insisting she be there. The panel's Tuesday afternoon, Orlando Civic Center."

Shelley stood, appointment book clutched to her chest and protest lodged in her throat. She could not go back to Orlando yet. No! Not yet! Dirk would find her. She was not ready for that.

As she stood, immobilized, Jerry looked up. "We're using that new hotel, the one connected to the Center. You may as well stay where the action is. Get Travel to book you into it." His attention went back to the material on his desk. "Oh, one more thing, he said, looking up, "The programs are already printed so your name won't be in it. You'll have to make the announcement that you're taking Cathy Goddard's place before your panel starts its discussion."

Shelley didn't remember leaving Jerry's office, but here she was, seated at her desk, heart pounding. Taking a deep breath, she forced her good sense to come to the fore. Dirk wouldn't be in Orlando! Get real, Shelley, she chastised herself. Dirk is a Miami lawyer. He has commitments. He has appointments. He has court dates. He is not going to pursue some insignificant technical editor. He is so handsome in his darkly piratical way, he could have any woman he wanted. How could he possibly love her?

That settled to her dissatisfaction, she sat down to work.

In the last editorial planning session, she had picked up three assignments. She had a new product to review; one of their free-lancers had submitted a highly technical report and she had to edit it and validate the art work. Thirdly, she found herself caught behind a "how-to" article. Fortunately, it was in an area of her expertise and would not pose a problem.

Saturday and Sunday passed rapidly. The two days off caused by the storm kept everyone working steadily. There was nothing like a looming deadline for building tension. They were almost too busy for the usual joking around that relieved it. Occasionally Shelley found herself gazing into space, caught in memories of her time with Dirk. She would snap back, finding herself shivering at the remembered touch of his kisses, the powerful way he had carried her across the sand, or the highly romantic moment on the beach at Southernmost Point. She would not allow herself to think of anything that had happened after he had thrust her into the bedroom and closed the door.

She worked through Monday, finally finishing her portion of the assignments. The hi-tech article had been changed from second person to third and the sentence structure now conformed to the style of the magazine. The copy editor had been sent all three pieces, but somebody else would have to go over the 'hyphenated and justified' file and check the page proofs. She hoped Sandy could do that tomorrow. She would talk to her on the way out.

Two hundred fifty miles was a long way to drive after the demanding week and a half she had experienced. It was a grueling five hours to Orlando and she still had to stop at her condo. She was pleased she thought of packing her few clothes that morning. Sandy had not wanted her to leave. It had been like old times in school and she had kissed her good-bye when she left. There really was no reason not to stay in Orlando once her stint in the trade show was finished.

She had reminded herself on the way down that she needed to get some changes of clothing. Casual clothes were all right in the office. The men even wore sport shirts, although jeans were frowned upon. The trade shows were different. Women wore suits or career-type dresses. The men wore shirts and ties, sometimes removing their jackets. Usually the companies whose products were reviewed were represented as well as the manufacturers of hardware. It was imperative that a professional image be projected. They were the ambassadors for *Strategic Computing* and had to dress the part.

It took Shelly twenty minutes from the time she parked the car in her slot at the condo until she drove out again. She paid no attention to the car that pulled in behind her and kept pace as she drove to the Civic Center Hotel.

The driver of the car watched as Shelly gave her Cabriolet to the valet and carried her garment bag up to the beautifully paneled and lushly planted foyer. He reached for his car-phone, prepared to call the list of numbers to give Dirk Gentile his latest report.

In the lobby the soothing sound of the two-story waterfall overrode the bustle of the busy area. Shelley's eyes followed the glass elevator's climb on the inside wall of the 20-story atrium as she walked to the registration desk.

After receiving her plastic key/card, she stopped by the Bell Captain's desk to ask him to have a sandwich and coffee sent to her room. Slipping the strap to the garment bag over her shoulder, she crossed to the elevator. There in the lobby, prominently displayed, was a sign welcoming the FBA, and their guests from the ABA. Shelley was exhausted and her eyes merely drifted over the message. The ding of the bell announcing the elevator doors closing shook her into acknowledging what she thought she had seen. She started toward the door just as it closed and the elevator began its noiseless ascent. Turning to the glass wall, she could see the sign rapidly sinking below her.

'Florida Bar Association'? Guests from the 'American Bar Association"? Was she hallucinating? That must be it! Dirk was on her mind so much that she was imagining the 'FBA' on the board. After all, how many coincidences does it take to make a fairy tale?

Although Shelley was overtired and spent a restless night, she was up early. She showered, dressed, and was at breakfast by 7:30. She ate in the courtyard of the atrium, the wrought iron tables and chairs lending the effect of an outdoor garden.

While waiting to be served, Shelley saw several guests wandering down a concourse leading to a shopping arcade. She marked that for future reference, then idly glanced at the folder placed on the table. From the information given, it seemed one could live here cocooned from the outside in a self-contained world. The pictures of the Health Club and swimming pool were so attractive, she decided to visit them as soon as her stint at the panel discussion was finished. Ten days of tension needed release in a strenuous workout.

She stopped in the hospitality rooms, drinking coffee, greeting old acquaintances, and meeting people who were formerly faceless voices on the phone. She was thrilled when several people approached her and introduced themselves, recognizing her picture from her column heading in the magazine, and commented favorably on her articles.

Leaving the hospitality room, she collided with a clown carrying a colorful bouquet of balloons and a sign with a reminder to attend the cocktail party and reception to be given that evening by one of the leading software companies. She smiled at him as he pantomimed how sorry he was, and went off to check the Flagler Room where her panel was to meet. She slid into one of the back rows to formulate what she hoped would be stimulating questions for the panelists. She drew on her article for her introductory talk.

The panelists were another story. She had been given the program when she had registered, and while she knew two of the participants listed, she needed more background material on the other two.

On the way to the publicity room, she stopped in the Hemingway Room where the Society for Applied Learning Technology was conducting a workshop on the information and delivery systems that were planned for Health Services. Leaving as quietly as she had entered, she wandered into the ballroom.

It was instant chaos: music, lights, movement, color. The large computer companies had booths and were handing out literature and samples. Software companies were discussing programs and giving demonstrations. Computer magazines and newsletters were enrolling subscribers. One booth was offering information on the packaging and shipping of critical materials. Another offered more labels for sale than Shelley had ever seen. In the center aisle, crystal bowls of ice sat on tables that offered participants non-alcoholic drinks and coffee.

When a waiter dropped a tray of glasses and ice, the tremendous crash caused a hush to fall over the room. It seemed as if people were momentarily frozen in time. A prickling sensation caused Shelley to look across the ballroom. Her heart leapt in her chest, her mouth went dry, and her knees trembled. No! It could not be! She was hallucinating again. Dirk could be at the Bar Association meeting, but no way would he be wandering around in the circus-like atmosphere of a computer trade show.

As movement returned to the room and the noise level climbed, Shelley moved to open the exit door behind her. It led to a carpeted, partially deserted corridor. She looked frantically around her. She could not go to her room. This time she was registered under her own name and would be easy to trace.

She ran for her car. She had to get away for a few minutes. It was difficult to pretend to be invisible while she waited for the valet to bring her car, but she did her best. Thrusting a bill into the valet's hand, she peeled away from the hotel. In the rearview mirror, she could see the horrified look on the valet's face as he stared at the black strips of rubber on the new concrete driveway.

Slowing down to a sedate 35, Shelley drove to one of Orlando's beautiful parks and left her car at the curb. She walked over to sit on the bank at the edge of a sparkling pond. Ducks and geese glided sedately by, triangular wakes following close behind them. As the birds swam tranquilly about, Shelley's insides began to compose themselves. There was no way she could avoid moderating that panel. There was also no way Dirk could locate her there. Her name was not on the program! That was one wonderful favor to be thankful for.

O.K., planning session again! She would eat lunch in one of the fast food places near the park. Except she was sure not a morsel would pass her lips. Well, maybe her lips—but she'd never be able to swallow.

O.K., next! She would bribe one of the maids to get her briefcase from her room and meet her in the hall behind the Flagler Room. Yes, that would work. Surely the maid could also show her which door led to the stage. Shelley nodded her head. Yes. She'd stay away from the well-traveled areas. She hated skulking about and peeping around corners, but if that's what she had to do, well . . . that's what she'd do.

Shelley returned to the hotel feeling calm and noble. Yes, noble, as in 'Noblesse oblige!' She was coming back to do her duty under great personal stress! But, this time, she would park her car in the underground garage. This time, she'd know where her car was, and she could pick it up herself without waiting at the front entrance. Everything went according to plan. The panel discussion was well received and invited lively participation from the audience. There were two gentlemen who nearly came to blows over freedom of information versus protection by copyright, but they ended up smiling sheepishly and shaking hands.

Just as Shelley was wrapping up the program, the prickling of her scalp caused her to raise her eyes. Dirk was standing in the back of the room, leaning against the wall, arms folded impassively across his chest.

Shelly stood, calmly collected her papers, closed her briefcase, and turned to walk off stage. From the comer of her eye, she saw Dirk straighten as he realized what she planned to do. He tried valiantly to cut through the audience, all of whom were chatting amiably as they flowed toward the doors.

By the time Dirk had worked his way backstage, Shelley was long gone. She had scuttled out of the room, dashed for the elevator, and was safely locked in her room.

However, the night before, Al had been nothing if not efficient. After he had followed Shelley from her condo to the Civic Center Hotel and phoned Dirk, he had ambled in to the desk, flashed his investigator's badge, and asked for Shelley's room number, having made up some plausible story to go with the request. When Dirk hit town, the room number was available for him.

Using that information, Dirk took the elevator to the seventh floor. When he reached Shelley's room, he knocked gently at the door. She made use of the security peephole to discover it was Dirk knocking.

"Shelly, love," Dirk called softly, "Open the door. It's Dirk, Shelley." He continued knocking. "Please, love, let me in. Let me apologize."

Shelly had mixed emotions about letting him in. Although she loved him, the feeling of betrayal was still with her. She knew she was not ready to face him yet. Nervously, she moved further back in the room and waited for him to leave.

In a few minutes the phone rang. She did not answer it, but the strain of hearing it ring ten times was very wearing. By then she was wringing her hands and pacing the floor.

After a pause, the telephone began ringing again. To escape the sound Shelley walked out on the balcony. The gentle breeze lifted the tendrils of hair that were sticking warmly to her face and neck. She stood breathing deeply as she let the view of the greenery in the gardens below calm her.

When the phone ceased ringing, she walked back into the room, sinking into a lounge chair and resting her head against the back. The exhilaration of the trade show, the pressure of the panel, the lack of sleep the night before, and finally, Dirk's appearance, had Shelley drained. She was starting to drift off to sleep when the knocking began again.

"Shelley!" Dirk called between knocks. "Shelly, open the door! Answer me! I know you're in there! Open the door!" As he continued to knock loudly, several doors along the corridor opened. It was evident from the stares of the guests that they were being disturbed. Dirk turned on his heel and headed for the stairwell just about the time Shelley had decided to open the door.

Grateful to see that he had left, she began pacing again. How could Dirk do this? Why couldn't he leave her alone? How could a man keep a woman in his home, a virtual prisoner, in today's world, and claim it was love? In her family, love allowed freedom, love set no boundaries, because love was unselfish.

Shelley threw herself into a chair and gazed into space. Maybe she should talk to Dirk. They had never discussed this problem; they had never discussed it openly. Perhaps he should have a chance to present his side. He <u>had</u> said he wanted to apologize.

As she sat there in the gathering twilight, two sharp knocks on the door shook her from her reverie. Leaping up like a startled fawn, she stood frozen in place, staring at the door. Two more sharp knocks were accompanied by a strange voice saying, "Miss Morgan? Flowers, Miss Morgan."

She walked softly to the door and checked through the fisheye lens of the peephole. She could see up and down the corridor, but in front of the door, all she could see was a huge flower arrangement being held by someone in gold striped trousers and patent leather shoes.

"Who is it?" she asked in a quavering voice.

The bouquet was moved slightly aside. "It's the bellman, Miss Morgan. A delivery from the flower shop."

"Is there anyone with you?"

"With me? No, ma'am."

Dear God! She sounded paranoid. She had to snap out of this.

"Just a moment, please." she called. She grabbed a bill from her purse and extended it as she opened the door.

"Thank you, but it's all taken care of, Miss Morgan. "Let me carry them in for you."

"Thank you, no. I can manage," she said as she peered nervously up and down the hall. Reaching for the arrangement, she backed hurriedly into the room and closed the door.

She carried the beautiful flowers over to set them on the dresser. It was a magnificent arrangement of tropical blooms accented by three brilliantly colored birds-of-paradise. Shelley caught her breath in admiration.

Somehow she was not surprised to find, "My love, Dirk," on the card. She sank to the edge of the bed and stared at them. There was no getting away from it, she would have to let him in. They had to talk.

Although Shelley had inspected the corridor, Dirk had been there. He had pulled hastily out of sight when she opened the door. Which solved one thing for him: Shelley was in her room! He had begun to have his doubts, but now he could put Phase II in operation.

Shortly afterward, there was another set of knocks at Shelley's door and she checked through the safety aperture in the door. She could see a silver champagne bucket, draped in a pristine white napkin, with a wine bottle extending beyond the rim. No person was visible.

To her query, "Who is it?", a disembodied voice answered, "Wine Steward.' Not again, she thought to herself. Visions of a video she had seen of the *Twelve Days of Christmas* flashed through her mind, and for a mad moment she envisioned twelve flower arrangements, eleven wine buckets, and who knew what else.

Her nervous titter brought her back to her room on the seventh floor. She opened the door and reached for the wine bucket. She found herself gently, but firmly, pushed inside the room, the wine bucket set on the floor, and the door firmly closed.

"Dirk," she breathed.

"Shelley, please listen to me," Dirk pleaded as he reached for her.

She stepped beyond his reach and walked quickly toward the balcony. She turned to face him when she approached the French doors, her hands raised, palms outward. "Stay there, Dirk. Talk to me from there. I can't think when you're too close to me."

Dirk turned to walk toward the door leading to the corridor, his right hand rubbing the back of his neck, the other on his hip forcing his jacket back. He turned to face her.

Her eyes filled with tears. How could she still love him? But she did. And she'd listen. But she wasn't making herself, or Dirk, any promises.

"Shelley, love, I've been worried sick about you. No one would tell me where you were. It was as if you'd dropped off the face of the earth." He turned toward the door and straightened his shoulders. "I don't think I could handle that. I don't think I could live without you."

Shelley's breath caught in her throat. Somehow that was not what she had expected him to say.

When he turned back to face her, there was a glint of moisture beneath his eyes. Noting the tears sparkling in her eyes, he took a step toward her. "Ah, Shelley love, please don't cry. Tell me what I need to do."

Shelley shook her head. "You don't have to do anything except understand how betrayed I felt when I found you'd tricked me."

Dirk moved a step closer. "I only wanted you to stay with me long enough to learn to love me. I love you so much. I thought if you learned to love me then you'd never leave me." He turned to walk back toward the corridor. This time his left hand rubbed the back of his neck and his right hand was jammed in his pocket.

When he turned to her again, both hands were in his pockets and he stared at the floor. "I realize I acted like some sort of primitive. Believe me when I tell you I'm more surprised at my behavior than you are." He smiled sheepishly. "Hollis read me the riot act. My dad couldn't have done it better." He looked at the ceiling. "He was right, too. I <u>was</u> selfish, egocentric, I think he inferred 'spoiled brat'."

"How did you find me?" she asked. "Were you at the Bar Association meeting?"

"No. It had gone completely out of my mind. No. A friend of mine, a private investigator, was watching for you to return to your condominium. He followed you to the hotel, then phoned me. I flew up from Miami this morning."

"You had me followed?" Shelley whirled to face the doors. "I can't believe this. You had me 'staked out' like a common criminal?"

When she turned back to the room, Dirk was in front of her. Reaching for her, he breathed, "I love you, Shelley. Believe anything else you want, but be aware that I love you." He clasped her to him and relaxed as he felt her melt against him. "I apologize for acting so uncivilized," he murmured.

"You did rather act like a throwback to the pirates in your family," she answered.

Ignoring the truth of her statement, he held her closer, letting his hands run lovingly over her back and shoulders. "We made such beautiful memories together, Shelley love. I'm sure we can work everything out as long as we love each other."

"I love you, Dirk," Shelley said as she snuggled closer to him, "But we do have more talking to do." He pressed her against his body until every muscle and bone imprinted itself on her soft curves. The tighter he held her, the more he desired her. He was burning hot, his arms like crushing steel bands.

The warmth of his breath wafted over her lips and his musky scent tantalized her as he bent to press his lips to hers. Shelley could think of nothing but how wonderful it felt to be in his arms again, drowning in his kisses.

He pressed damp, open-mouthed kisses along the cords of her neck. The sound of the zipper on her dress was a distant buzz as he lowered her to the bed. His rough cheeks burned against her own smooth ones. He murmured soft, heated endearments as he gently bit her earlobes. Slowly he removed the rest of her clothing. Leaving her for a moment, he removed his own and sank to the bed beside her. His voice telling of his love was like a caress of velvet sliding over sensitive skin. "Mine," he whispered as his kisses traveled along her body. "I'm yours, but you're mine. You belong to me."

They would discuss that later, Shelley thought dazedly, but for now, in this time, in this room, she was definitely and delightedly—his!

*　　*　　*　　*　　*

Still smiling Shelley was aware of Dirk's entry into the room with their three beautiful adolescent daughters. She turned to him and as he neared her side, a little grayer, but still stunningly good looking, she was so pleased that she was still very much in love with him. A warm glow rose inside her as he kissed her tenderly on her cheek.

"Mom—the zoo was great! We saw such creatures you wouldn't believe it!" Maggie exploded.

"I can't believe how cool it was. And to think we didn't want to go . . . ," Celeste allowed.

"I believe it! I still love the zoo, too," Shelley smiled.

"We're gonna go tell Nuncie all about it and nab some chow. Bye, Mom! Bye, Daddy, thanks!" yelled Lillie over her shoulder as Maggie and Celeste nodded.

Dirk tousled their hair as they ran from the terrace. "So, you were looking dreamy. It appeared we interrupted you. What were you thinking about?" asked Dirk.

"Oh, just some crazy whirlwind days seventeen years ago."

Dirk chuckled.

They turned to the setting sun, arms entwined about each other's waists and sighed deeply. And then they saw it—the green flash! Shelley startled in surprise. Dirk squeezed Shelley ever more tightly and smiled. But then, he already knew he was the luckiest man alive.

A romantic's romantic, Rosemary Austin was married for 60 years to her deeply loved and loving husband, Glenn. Her writing reflects her optimism, and her belief in deep abiding love and good plain fun. Living in several parts of the United States and a world-wide traveler, Florida was one of her favorite haunts. In Tell Me No Lies, she captures perfectly a sunny week in Florida as two people fatefully meet and struggle against each other into love. She had three other novels in various stages of writing, but slipped away before she finished them.